A GOOSE GIRL

Entwined Tales: Volume 1

K. M. SHEA

A GOOSE GIRL

Cover design by Page Nine Media

Edited by Jeri Larsen

www.kmshea.com

ISBN: 978-1-950635-05-4

❀ Created with Vellum

WORLD OF ENTWINED TALES

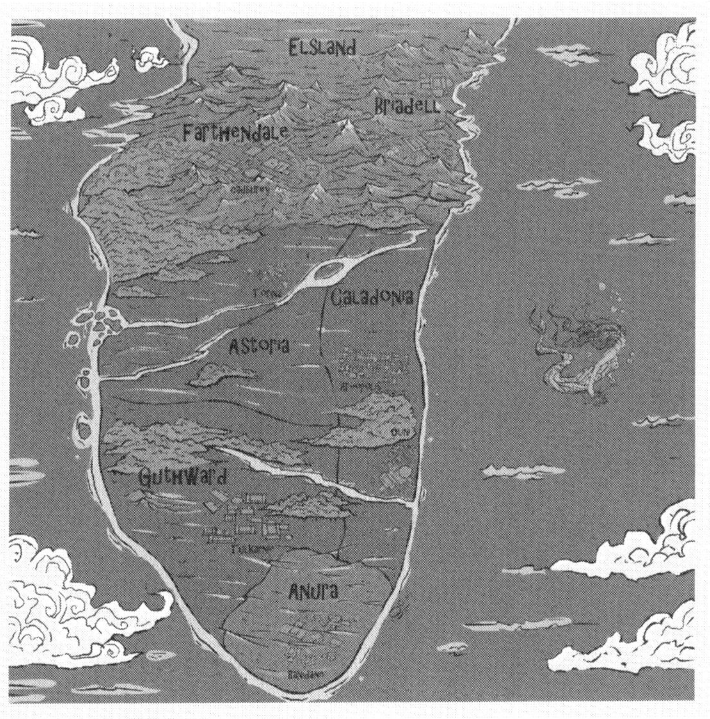

CHAPTER 1
A POOR PLAN

"Corynn...have you ever wanted to be *more*?" Princess Davina asked.

"No," Rynn replied without hesitation.

"You didn't let me finish!" the princess complained. She jutted her lower lip out and batted her eyelashes, adopting a pouting expression that managed not to ruin her beauty.

Rynn sighed and absently patted her horse when it did the same. "I apologize, Princess. What were you going to say?"

Satisfied, Princess Davina nodded once. "Haven't you ever wanted to be more than a lady's maid? Perhaps...did you ever wish to be a princess?"

"*No*," Rynn said even faster than the first time.

Princess Davina furrowed her delicate brow. "Why not?"

"Because I had a difficult enough time managing my siblings before I came to work for you, Princess. I can't imagine it would be any easier to manage an entire country," Rynn said.

Princess Davina flinched when her horse—a beautiful gelding whose coat glittered like the stars and whose mane and tail were white as snow—pinned its ears and chewed audibly on its bit.

"Oh, being a princess is not that much work, really," she said. "Most days, everyone tells you what to do!"

"Mmhmm," Rynn said. She turned in her saddle to glance back at the four soldiers who rode behind them. Three of them rode their horses in a languishing manner, yawning and slumping in their saddles. The last—Captain Hulderic, who led the squad—drove a covered cart that was laden with gems, gold, costly fabrics, and more. He smiled when he met Rynn's gaze. Though it was a pleasant gesture, it didn't cancel out the consistently-narrowed look to his eyes.

Rynn ignored her desire to frown sharply. *Captain Hulderic aside, such a* fine *guard the queen sent to escort her eldest daughter to her future home and husband. What possessed her to choose such men?*

"Personally, I always wished to be a rich heiress," Princess Davina continued.

"You *are* a rich heiress, Princess," Rynn pointed out.

"No, no, no. I mean the rich heiresses you hear about in the stories—the ones who are free to travel as they so choose and eat grapes off of golden platters served by handsome male attendants." Princess Davina smiled dreamily.

Rynn ignored the princess's daydreams. *She's always been a romantic thinker. It's no surprise she would be especially...dreamy, given that she's traveling as a bride to a new country.*

Princess Davina's marriage was part of an agreement between Astoria—the princess's country—and Farthendale. The princess's mother, Queen Cassia, had made the arrangements to assure harmony between the two countries. While Astoria and Farthendale were economically dependent on each other, they did not have the smoothest of relationships. Naturally, this meant Princess Davina had complained about her future nearly every step of the journey.

I will not allow her to turn this lovely afternoon into another pity party for herself. Rynn cleared her throat. "As a princess, you have a wonderful life. Your mother has never spared an expense to see to your happiness. I imagine your fiancé in Farthendale will treat you with the same adoration." (It was likely, given that Princess Davina was astonishingly beautiful, even if she was a bit empty-headed.)

Princess Davina placed a delicate hand over her heart. "No, do not say it. You cannot remind me of the dark future that awaits me! In Farthendale, the royal family eats with their fingers and doesn't even have a *tablecloth* covering their banquet table, and the civilians let their goats live indoors with them. They hate music, and—worse yet—Prince Geraint has a hunchback and squints!"

Ahh, yes. She would *be most concerned about the prince's appearance.* "Might I ask who served as your source of this information?" Rynn asked.

"The chambermaid said she heard from her mother's cousin, whose neighbor is a merchant who ships to Farthendale," Princess Davina said.

Rynn rolled her eyes. "In summary, such tales are nothing more but rumors. And rumors often say the worst about everyone."

"They could have a grain of truth," Princess Davina said.

"Princess, we're traveling in Farthendale lands right now," Rynn pointed out. "The citizens we have met thus far are all as cheerful and kind as the Astorians back home."

"It doesn't matter," Princess Davina said bleakly as tears welled up in her lovely blue eyes. "Farthendale could be the most beautiful place on earth—which it won't be—and I would still hate it. I so long to have no cares at all and to be free to do as I wish," Princess Davina continued.

"Idiot," the princess's white horse growled.

Both Davina and Rynn winced.

The princess's horse, Falada, was a fairy steed that had been given to the Astorian royal family as a gift from the fairies themselves. He was a mark of their distinguishment.

Given Falada's rather black-hearted temperament, ability to

speak, and proneness to throwing his rider, Rynn often thought the gift was perhaps more of curse. But in her own family's experience, magic often *was* rather temperamental.

Pushed into silence by the ornery fairy horse, the lady's maid and princess quietly rode down the dirt road. Rynn didn't mind. As she had spent most of her life in Astoria's golden plains, Farthendale's plentiful forests and mountains were wonderous to behold.

It was almost an hour before the princess dared to speak again. "May we stop?" she asked. "I should like to go to the river and drink some refreshing water."

"I will fetch water for you. I can use the gold chalice your mother gave you," Rynn said.

"Oh, you don't have to—"

"I *insist*." Rynn halted her horse and slipped off its back. *If I let her off that horse, it will be hours before I can get her back on!* The journey had already dragged on longer than it should have, and Rynn was eager to drop Davina off in Farthendale so she could return to Astoria and clear herself of all responsibilities for the princess. "It is my duty as your maid."

Princess Davina smiled and again placed her hand over her heart. "You are so devoted to me. I am so glad to have a maid worthy of me," she declared. She yipped a little when her fairy horse snorted deeply enough to rock his whole body, even though he had stopped as well.

Rynn smiled at the princess, nodded to the guards who had lazily stopped behind them, and dug out the gold cup from her saddle bag before marching to the river that gurgled and chirped just behind a screen of trees and bushes.

She glanced over her shoulder, slightly surprised to see Princess Davina nudge her horse closer to Captain Hulderic and call out to him.

Captain Hulderic is a night watchman. I did not think she would know him. Rynn shrugged and ducked a branch. She scrambled across the sandy shore and walked into the river—hissing a little at its cold temperature. She took the opportunity to drink some water herself before carefully filling the chalice with clear water. (Even a grain of sand would be enough to make Davina send Rynn back for a new cupful.)

When she was finally satisfied, Rynn trekked back through the trees, shielding the cup and moving carefully lest she spill the water.

Princess Davina smiled as Rynn rejoined the party on the road. "Thank you, Corynn." She reached down to take the chalice from Rynn—who backed away as soon as the trade-off was made. (If she lingered, Falada might decide to take a chunk out of her hide. Again.)

"I was just telling Captain Hulderic how loyal you are," Princess Davina continued. She sipped her water and bequeathed a gentle smile on Rynn. "You would do much for my sake, wouldn't you?"

"I do my best to serve the Astorian royal family," Rynn said, which was the gentlest way she knew to say "not really." (The princess's desires were often opposed to the Queen's, whom Rynn considered far more important.)

Captain Hulderic smiled first at Davina then at Rynn. "You two do seem close."

Princess Davina nodded eagerly. "Indeed! Could we not be mistaken for sisters?"

"*Hah*!" The snort of disbelief escaped Rynn before she could smack her hand over her mouth. With Davina's bright blue eyes on her, Rynn coughed. "I beg your pardon—there was a tickle in my throat."

"I do hope you feel better now. But, Captain, don't you agree with me? Do we not look alike?" Davina asked.

Rynn turned her back to the pair so she could remount her horse and roll her eyes.

Davina and Rynn looked about as alike as any set of strangers one could stumble upon. Yes, they both had blonde hair, but where Davina's was sunshine yellow, Rynn's was a darker shade of amber. Davina's blue eyes were never more menacing than a shade of summer sky, but Rynn's were a perpetual storm-cloud gray. Moreover, Rynn was at least a hand taller, and while the princess moved like a deer, Rynn had the quick but efficient movements of a work horse.

Captain Hulderic shared Rynn's eye for realism, though he was rather polite about it. "Perhaps one could mistake the two of you to have a sister-like bond?"

Davina dropped the chalice in her dismay. (Which meant Rynn had to dismount and retrieve it.) "Oh, but we look so alike!" Tears began pooling in the princess's wide eyes, and her lower lip trembled.

"Of course you do," Captain Hulderic said in a soothing tone. "The pair of you look more alike than you and the Queen herself." He sounded so genuine, it took Rynn a moment to realize his sanity had not, in fact, left him, and instead he was merely lying to the princess.

He's a smooth deceiver, Rynn noted as she snatched the chalice up and retreated back to her mount.

Princess Davina sniffed. "Thank you, Captain. Your words are very kind."

Rynn's forehead puckered as she once again clambered back into the saddle. *Why does the princess suddenly care if we look alike? She prizes her appearance and hates to be told anyone comes near to her in beauty.*

"It is my pleasure, Princess." Captain Hulderic bowed from his seat on the cart, making Davina giggle.

"If you have finished *prattling*," Falada-the-frightening-fairy-horse said in a voice of rusted metal. "Are we not ready to move along, or do you need help dismounting?"

Princess Davina turned pale as Falada pranced in place in an obvious threat to buck her off. "We are ready!" she squeaked.

Falada proceeded, setting the pace at a swifter walk than it had been.

Shivering slightly, Rynn and the soldiers followed.

❧

THE FOLLOWING DAY found Rynn rather puzzled, for the princess was so giddy, she hummed all morning—until Falada turned his head and bared his teeth at her.

"I am glad to see your mood has improved, Princess," Rynn said. She gazed at the forest, listening to the sound of foreign birds chirping and the gurgle of the river—which was still audible.

"Of course!" Princess Davina said. "Soon I will step into my long-awaited future!"

"I thought you did not want to marry Prince Geraint?" Rynn asked.

Princess Davina, who had been smiling up at the strip of sky they could see through the impossibly tall trees, stiffened. "Yes, well, I believe deeply in the luck of my family!"

As the same luck had also bestowed Falada on them, Rynn suspected the belief was rather mistaken, but she was not going to sour the princess's mood when she had sulked nearly the entire journey.

"I see." Rynn shifted in her side-saddle and adjusted her horse's reins.

The sound of horse hooves drifted through the forest, and soon after, one of the soldiers mounted on a lathered horse careened around a bend in the road. He pulled his horse to a walk and saluted. "Sir, Princess, Cadburey lies but an hour ahead of us."

"Well done, soldier," Captain Hulderic praised.

Princess Davina squealed. "A mere hour! How exciting! Captain—it is time, is it not?"

Rynn blinked. "Time for what, Princess?"

Captain Hulderic made a show of rubbing his chin and

studying the princess. "Are you sure this is what you want, Princess Davina?"

For a moment, Rynn's heart stopped. *What is he saying? She can't possibly back out of the marriage!*

"Indeed," Davina said, relieving Rynn.

"You will come to love Farthendale as much as you love Astoria, Princess," Rynn said.

Davina smiled and pulled back on the reins, making Falada sneer. "I'm afraid it won't matter." She slipped from her saddle, a beaming smile settled on her face.

Rynn frowned and was quick to dismount. "What are you talking about?" She grabbed her horse's reins, toting it behind her as she followed Davina to the cart filled with her dowry.

Davina pushed back the burlap sacks that covered the cart's precious cargo. "It is time for me to finally live out my dreams and travel as a rich heiress."

A throbbing headache began to carve its way into Rynn's skull. *I left my parents and six siblings because I thought it would be easier to manage one princess than the lot of them. I was incredibly misguided.* "Princess, you cannot be serious."

"But I am! I have spent nights planning my escape." Davina snagged two beautiful saddlebags that sported gold leafing and embroidery from the spot directly behind Captain Hulderic's seat. She opened the flap, briefly revealing the gold coins, pearls, and jewelry that filled the saddlebags.

Rynn glanced up at Captain Hulderic, hoping he would speak to Davina—or at least stop her! She was encouraged when he climbed off the cart, until he picked up the saddlebags and carried them towards Rynn's mount.

"Captain," Rynn hissed as she scrambled to keep up with him. "You must stop this!"

He shrugged. "I cannot say no to the princess."

"*Yes, you can*!" Rynn hissed.

Captain Hulderic slung the saddle pack over Rynn's horse and tied it to the saddle. "As a soldier sworn to her family, I wish for Princess Davina's happiness."

"The princess's happiness must take second priority to the good of Astoria!" Rynn snapped. She turned to Davina, hoping she could talk some sense into the girl! *If Davina shirks her duty, it will surely cause trouble for our countries, but if I have to face Queen Cassia and inform her I let Davina waltz off, I will be imprisoned!* "Princess, you must think this through! If you do not travel to Farthendale and marry Prince Geraint, you will throw into disarray the uneasy alliance upon which our countries have agreed."

"I know." Princess Davina nodded with great solemnity. She then turned and rested a hand on Rynn's shoulder. "Which is why you shall go in my stead."

Rynn was fish-mouthed in her shock. "*What?*" she finally shrieked.

"You will travel to Farthendale and pretend to be me, taking over my life as a princess. Though you'll have to change first to make it at all believable. I would never let this shabby drab you call a dress touch my skin." Davina rubbed the sleeve of Rynn's traveling dress between her fingers.

Rynn didn't know what to say—she was too stunned by all of the obvious problems with the plans. *Is there no end to this girl's stupidity?* "Princess, I cannot pretend to be you. We look nothing alike, and when Prince Geraint discovers our betrayal, it will *certainly* sever Astoria's relationship with Farthendale!"

Davina pushed her luxurious blonde hair over her shoulder. "How can he find out? Neither he nor anyone from the royal family has met me in person."

"But several Farthendale ambassadors have met you," Rynn said. "Moreover, your mother promised to visit. *She* will know I am not you!"

"Oh, pooh," Princess Davina sniffed. "You can tell the ambassadors a fairy had cast a temporary spell on you to make you unbelievably beautiful. I *am* stunning enough for it to be believed, and Farthendale's boring, mountain-stock, clod-pole people see less magic in a full year than we Astorians do in a single day."

Rynn shook her head, barely holding back the desire to strangle the impulsive princess. "And your mother?"

Davina's bright smile faded, and she stared unseeingly at the second saddle pack Captain Hulderic positioned over Rynn's horse's haunches. "Please, Corynn. I know you think me tiresome, but even I am not so dull as to believe my mother—or my little brothers—will ever come visit me."

Rynn hesitated, her heart softening at the emptiness of Davina's gaze. *Wait, no, she is still proposing a stupidly* selfish *idea!* "Even if they do not, Princess, Lady Maela, the Astorian ambassador to Farthendale, knows you. She will tell the king."

"She will do no such thing." Davina laughed gaily. "She *helped* me plan this."

The Astorian royal family needs to better investigate the loyalties of their people. Desperately, Rynn said, "There will be other visitors from Astoria. They will know!"

Davina shrugged. "You're clever; I'm certain you will figure it out."

"No, I won't," Rynn clenched her teeth and raised her chin. "Because I will not take part in this. When the soldiers and I return to Astoria, we will tell your mother *everything*!"

"Actually, they won't." Captain Hulderic smiled pleasantly, almost *smugly*.

"Indeed! I have given them each a small allotment from my dowry—except for Captain Hulderic, that is. *He* understands my grievances," Davina declared.

Rynn shook her head. "No, they would not shirk so poorly in their duties." She glanced at the three soldiers who lingered near the cart.

The soldier who had ridden ahead shrugged. "The princess paid us off before we set out on the journey."

"I sought Captain Hulderic's help long before we left. It was why I specifically asked Mother that he and a few of his men would serve as my guards on the journey," Davina said, sounding proud.

The revelation was like a bucket of ice water dumped over Rynn, and she backed away, eyeing Captain Hulderic anew. *He might claim he is doing this for Davina's sake, but to go through such deception? And to willingly have such disloyal men in his service? That's not something an honorable captain would do.*

Still, Rynn could not be cowed. While her foremost concern was the country—and yes, she was more than a little worried about what would happen to *her*—she knew Davina. The princess would come to ruin within days of her little charade. She was too easy to trust and far too innocent to survive without help. (Though this episode *was* making Rynn rethink that assumption.)

"You cannot make me fill your place. I will return to Astoria even if I must walk the whole way, and I will reveal what you've done," Rynn said.

"You will go to Farthendale," Davina said.

Rynn shook her head. "I will not."

"You will," Davina said. "The good Captain Hulderic will see that you do."

Hulderic smiled, though his fingers lingered on the hilt of his sword. "I have no wish to harm you, Corynn," he said. "But I will do what I must for the princess's sake."

Rynn was not fooled by his noble-sounding words. *There is something else at play here—something more than Davina's selfish plans.* Warily, she backed up a step. Her eyes flickered between the captain and the princess as the captain drew his sword.

She tried to run, but she slammed straight into one of the soldiers—who had dismounted and crept up behind her at some point during the conversation.

Rynn kneed him in the gut—which hurt her knee more than it hurt him, as she had rammed her leg into his armored belly.

The soldier laughed and snaked his arms around her. "By all means fight," he leered, his yellow teeth flashing behind his caterpillar lips. "Makes it more *exciting* for me!"

Rynn grit her teeth, then smashed her head into the soldier's nose, breaking it.

The soldier gave a muffled oath and released her as he staggered backwards, holding his nose.

Turning to run, Rynn froze when Captain Hulderic stepped smoothly in front of her and extended his sword so it brushed her throat.

Rynn gulped. She had been fairly certain she could fight a lazy, unprepared soldier. Against a sword, she did not have the same confidence. She glared at the captain first, then the princess. "Fine. You can truss me up and drag me kicking and screaming to Farthendale, but it won't matter. As soon as we arrive, I will tell them everything. You cannot keep me from uttering the truth!"

Davina smiled again—an expression Rynn was starting to despise. "Actually, I can." Davina pulled a white handkerchief from her bodice.

Rynn recognized it as the queen's parting gift to Davina—she had cut her finger and dribbled three drops of blood onto the cloth. Though the queen had given some grand speech about the princess carrying her heart with her represented by the droplets of blood, the gift had actually been in the cloth, not the blood.

For the handkerchief was of fairy weave and could be used to compel anyone into doing whatever the owner desired. It only worked once on each person, but once was all it would take.

Rynn swallowed, the coppery taste of desperation filling her mouth. *When I first came to work as a lady's maid...never did I ever imagine a day like this would arrive. What can I do? How can I get out of this mess?*

"Corynn," Davina began. "Neither you nor I will tell a single human soul in Farthendale who you really are. Neither of us will speak of our switch to anyone unless they are aware of who you really are, nor will you tell anyone where I am. You will go to Cadburey in my place and fulfill the role of princess."

Rynn squirmed as she felt the cloying, compelling fairy magic curl around her throat and tug on her hair and wondered if Davina was aware she was going to compel herself with the sloppy wording.

"Swear it," Davina ordered, holding up the cloth when Rynn said nothing.

Rynn clamped her mouth shut and started to cover her lips, until Captain Hulderic placed his blade against her throat with an apologetic expression. She snarled—much like Falada—as the words were unwillingly pulled from her lips. "I swear it."

The fairy magic seeped into her skin, though Rynn felt it click into place like an iron padlock. She scowled at Davina and Hulderic, already plotting ways around the vow. *What I would dearly like is to get my hands on that cloth and make the princess ride back to Astoria and confess to her mother what she has done!*

"Excellent!" Davina chirped. She drew closer to Rynn, ignoring Hulderic's sword—which he had not yet removed from Rynn's throat. Davina reached out and patted Rynn's hand. "It won't be so bad, Corynn. I dare say you will enjoy the life of a royal! Oh!"

Davina almost fell over when Rynn lunged at her, trying to pull the fairy cloth from her hands.

Hulderic slid between the girls smoothly, grabbing Rynn by the waist and hauling her backwards. "I would be careful with the cloth, Princess." Hulderic's tone was as kind and respectful as usual, even though Rynn tried to bite him. "Though she took the oath, I do not believe Corynn will give up quite so easily."

"Yes, I should dispose of it." Davina strode over to the river and peered at its frothy surface as water danced past.

Dispose of it? A fairy gift!? "Wait!" Rynn called too late.

The princess dropped the handkerchief in the water, and it was swept away.

Davina brushed her hands off and nodded—apparently not having realized she had just lost what would surely be a great boon to her in her travels as a "rich heiress."

I take it back. She won't even last a day!

Davina returned to the cart and ruffled through one of her trunks, unearthing a beautiful gown of gray-blue velvet. "Come. We'll get you changed into this and looking more proper."

Rynn was allowed to change behind a bush on the side of the road. She tried to flee—this was likely the only chance she would get. But whenever she took a step away from Cadburey, the fairy magic tightened around her neck like a noose and dragged her back towards the group.

Rynn was nearly shedding tears of frustration when she pushed her way through the bushes and rejoined the others, clutching her sensible dress and wearing the velvet gown.

I hate this! How can this be happening? Rynn scrubbed at her eyes, angry with herself for being duped and furious with Davina for being so blind and selfish.

Davina frowned. "You don't look nearly as beautiful as me, but I suppose it will have to do." She strode to Rynn's horse and swung up into the saddle. "With that, I believe all is settled! Thank you for your help, Captain Hulderic! You are ever so brave and chivalrous!" Davina turned the horse in a circle. "And Rynn, thank you. I know you wish to serve me—please know I appreciate this."

"I'm not doing this out of my own will, and I don't want to serve you!" Rynn struggled against Hulderic, who held her in an iron grip with ease. "What I want to do is slap your pretty face!"

Davina sighed dramatically and shook her head. "You don't understand, Corynn. I am a creature that is meant for freedom! Perhaps one day you shall see. Until then, farewell!" Davina kneed her horse, and they soon disappeared behind a bend in the forest road.

Rynn sagged in Hulderic's grip. *No. This can't be happening. This is a nightmare!*

"Come along, Corynn," the captain said.

Fear made Rynn's legs tremble, even as she forced herself to stand tall. "Please," she said. "How can you let her ride off like that? You must see the folly—the *danger*—in this! Princess Davina..."

"Is doing as she wishes." Captain Hulderic sheathed his sword, making Rynn breathe easier, until he pulled out a dagger the size of Rynn's forearm and rested it on her shoulder. "If you cooperate, you'll be fine," Captain Hulderic promised.

Goosebumps raised on Rynn's skin. Though the princess was triumphant that she had found men to help her, Rynn was growing more and more troubled by Hulderic's actions. *How could he go along with this as a servant to the crown? He does not seem to be addled by love for her, and if he is such a solid supporter of hers, I find it hard to believe he would let her waltz off without anyone to accompany her. So...why?*

Rynn's fear spiked when she realized Captain Hulderic was marching her towards Falada. "No! I'll stay with you in the cart—the spell Davina placed on me will keep me from running away. Just please, don't make me ride him!"

"I'm afraid everyone knows the princess rides a magic steed." Captain Hulderic's voice was pleasant and not at all concerned as they approached the beast who had maimed more men than Rynn had fingers. "You'll have to ride him to make the deception complete."

Though Rynn fought tooth and nail—trying everything from elbowing Hulderic in the throat to biting his nose—Hulderic soon had her boosted on top the white horse.

Falada pranced forward a few steps, crow-hopping the last one and snorting like an angry bull.

For one wild moment, Rynn thought he might break the formation and charge back to Astoria. Instead, he shook his head and made his bridle jingle. "Don't touch me," he growled. Another snort, and he started walking, the soldiers hurriedly throwing themselves on their horses so they could catch up.

Hot, miserable tears stung Rynn's eyes as a sense of betrayal twisted her heart. *What am I going to do? If the royal family of Farthendale recognizes our deception...what will happen?* Rynn shook her head and clenched her jaw almost as angrily as Falada. *And how could Davina do this?*

CHAPTER 2
THE ARRIVAL

Rynn's arrival in Farthendale was a boisterous and joyous event. A squadron of guards wearing their dress uniforms had lingered near the city gates—waiting for the Astorian Princess. When Hulderic presented a number of royal dispatches and proclamations to the guards—while Rynn mutely watched, unable to think of anything to do—the guards warmly greeted them and led them through the city.

Cadburey was built in tiers—like a cake—with trees sprouting out of rocky crevasses. It lacked the whimsical feeling of Astoria's capital, Torina, and Rynn didn't see any sign of merchants selling magical objects or even any shops boasting fairy goods. However, the woodworking that went into the buildings and furnishings was so ornate, Rynn would have thought they were carved by fairies themselves if it were not for the various craftsmen who puttered around their storefronts.

Rynn forced herself to smile and wave at the few citizens who paused in their work to watch the procession as they climbed their way up to the palace. *Unless they recognize outright that something is off, I don't have a choice but to play along...for now.* The gaping hole in Davina's order was that *if* someone figured out Rynn was a ceholder, she could confirm it. Most likely her best chance to eveal everything lay in getting someone to guess the truth.

Unfortunately, this meant Rynn would have to act as Davina for at least a few days, until she was able to discern who would best guess the situation. (It wouldn't do any good to try and goad Prince Geraint—Davina's fiancé—into guessing if he turned out to be as intelligent as Davina, after all.)

Falada chewed loudly on his bit and threw his head. Though he drew many eyes with his snowy coat, none of the soldiers dared to ride near them.

Several children shrieked in glee and ran along the side of the road, their arms wheeling wildly as they tried to jump a barrel. They missed and sent the barrel tilting over to its side and careening down the slanted road.

Many of the soldiers' mounts whinnied and shied away, but Falada snorted and charged towards the children.

Rynn both clung to the saddle and tried to rein the wild horse back in, but to no avail. *He's too strong!* "Falada—they're children; they meant no harm!"

Falada pawed at the edge of the road and eyed the children—who had fallen backwards and gaped up at the fairy horse. "You think I care?"

"I know it's been a long ride, but we're almost there. You're almost free," Rynn pleaded. She paused, then changed tactics. "Unless you'd rather be labeled a monster and locked up all day..." It was a method she had used often against Anneliese—one of the youngest of Rynn's many siblings.

Falada snorted, then turned away from the children and resumed chewing loudly on his bit.

Rynn almost toppled off his back in relief. With the moment of danger gone, she risked glancing at her escort, searching for the Astorian soldiers Davina had paid off. Captain Hulderic met her gaze and smiled, but he was the only one.

They're all useless! Not one of them tried to help! Rynn fought the desire to scowl and/or cry. *I'm alone in a new country, where—if I make a mistake—there might be country-sized consequences, and I can't even count on my fellow countrymen to keep me from breaking my neck on a horse!*

In that moment, Rynn missed her boisterous family and their beautiful home in Astoria. *I was so stupid to leave, no matter how they tried my patience. Now I don't know if I'll see any of them ever again...*

A trumpet pulled her from her thoughts as they passed through the great gates that separated the palace from the rest of the city.

"Announcing Her Royal Highness, Princess Davina of Astoria!" a soldier riding in front shouted.

Rynn's mouth turned dry as they picked their way through the courtyard and paused at the base of a grand staircase where—judging by the crowns—King Othmar, Queen Morgaine, and Prince Geraint waited.

Rynn glanced around before following the soldier's example and dismounting. Rather than approach the royal family, she hesitated at Falada's side. *Is it better to thank him as I would a person, or to stay silent to irritate him as little as possible?* After a few moments, her good manners won out, and Rynn murmured. "Thank you, Falada."

The horse studied her, his velvet muzzle twitching as he continued to angrily chomp on his bit.

She cleared her throat and let the magic of the vow Davina had forced on her drag her forward. It pulled on her like a chain around her neck, lessening only when Rynn reached the foot of the stairs.

Rynn had waited on Davina at enough court functions that she was reasonably aware of Astorian etiquette. So only her stomach twisted as she curtsied to the royal family. "Your Majesties," she murmured. She paused, but the magic ripped the unwilling words from her mouth, making her spit taste sour like bile. "I am Princess Davina—eldest of Queen Cassia of Astoria."

As soon as she declared the lie, the weight of the magic that clung to Rynn lessened. However, when Rynn opened her mouth to decry the lie, she found she couldn't speak. *This is so foul! I hope Davina gets a spider in her face while she rides!*

Queen Morgaine laughed. "Please, Davina. You are soon to be our daughter—formalities are not needed." The queen approached her and kissed her on the cheek. She was tall and stately with a hawkish nose and laughing eyes.

"Indeed," King Othmar said. "We must welcome you to the family, Davina!" When King Othmar joined her, Rynn was surprised to see the queen was actually taller than him. He was a very handsome man with deep smile lines and silver threaded through the temples of his chestnut-colored hair.

The king turned around and called to Prince Geraint. "Son, come greet your fiancée!"

Prince Geraint was as handsome as his father—though as his nose was perhaps more similar to his mother's, it gave him a rather dashing air—and his brown eyes reminded Rynn of the many forests they had ridden through.

Rynn could not help the smirk that briefly twitched across her lips. *No matter her prattle about freedom, if Davina knew Prince Geraint was so handsome, she'd be positively sulking!*

Another man who appeared to be of similar age to the prince lingered at his side for a moment before the two parted, and Prince Geraint joined his parents.

"Welcome to Farthendale, Davina," Prince Geraint said with a wide smile that made his eyes crinkle. "I hope you'll be happy here. With us." He glanced back at his previous companion—who flapped a hand at him—then bowed to Rynn.

Feeling like a fraud—no—*knowing* she was a fraud—Rynn managed a smile. "Thank you for the warm greeting."

"Your Majesties."

Rynn grimaced as Captain Hulderic smiled kindly—and emptily—and bowed to the monarchs. "I am Captain Hulderic—

the leader of the squad that brought Princess Davina here. I have some correspondences for you from Queen Cassia."

"Of course! Welcome, Captain. Thank you for bringing Davina here. I hope you and your men will stay for a time?" King Othmar asked.

Please leave soon! Please leave soon! If Hulderic wasn't around, Rynn would be able to move more recklessly in revealing the sham!

"My men will return shortly," the captain said. "But it was the queen's dearest wish I remain in service to the princess."

Rynn scowled. "What are you—"

"I have her orders in this letter, here." Captain Hulderic passed a satchel of letters to the king.

"Very well. If the queen and princess desire this, it would be our pleasure to welcome you to Farthendale," King Othmar declared as he took the satchel.

"Captain Hulderic," Rynn managed to say before the rest of the words died in her throat. *Blast! This must fall under the farce Davina described when she forbad me from speaking of it.* As much as it pained Rynn to admit, Davina's plan—though stupid—had been hatched with an uncommon amount of sense given the princess's usual aspirations. *I don't think I've ever seen her put this much effort into anything besides ordering new gowns! Unless Lady Maela helped her with all these details...*

Queen Morgaine curled an arm around Rynn's shoulders and swept her up the staircase. "Come; I will show you to your quarters! I imagine you wish for some time to yourself to rest after your journey, but tonight we shall throw a banquet in honor of your arrival."

"Thank you," Rynn said. "It is very kind of you, but you don't need to go through such trouble for *me*." She glanced first at the queen and then back at the king and prince—who climbed up the stairs behind them—but no one seemed to notice the syllable stress.

"Nonsense," the queen said. "You will be family, Davina!"

But I'm not Davina! Rynn tried to even whisper the words, but nothing could squeak out of her throat. Grimly, she tried to push back the dirty feeling that clung to her as she lied openly to the Farthendale monarchs. "Thank you, Your Majesty."

"Please, Davina, I said no formalities for our son's fiancée! You must call me Morgaine."

Rynn allowed herself to be pulled along, but she nursed rather rebellious thoughts. *If I ever get my hands on Davina, I'll throw her to the goats!*

❧

As Queen Morgaine had promised, that night the royal family held a banquet. Although Rynn had protested, a maid stuffed her in a beautiful ruby-red gown—which fit a bit oddly given that she was taller than Davina.

Rynn stared at her reflection in the mirror and tried not to cry. Though she had been working as Princess Davina's lady's maid for a year, she still saw her family frequently. She hadn't really worked many hours until her sister Eva, closest in age to her and also her best friend, had left the family home for the country of Guthward. Working had seemed like a wonderful escape—with Eva gone, she was left alone in her role of older sister—but now Rynn would have given anything to hear her sisters squabble and fight.

She tried to tug down the sleeves of her dress—which were supposed to end at the wrist but instead settled halfway up her forearm. (The skirt of the gown was also too short. Davina's wardrobe had been designed to have flowing skirts so her feet would never be seen as she glided along. On Rynn, they brushed the tops of her shoes.)

They're going to think Astorian royalty dress strangely. Rynn frowned at her dress and was prodded from her thoughts only when the maid interrupted her.

"Captain Hulderic has arrived to walk you to the celebration hall, Your Highness," the maid said.

Rynn whirled around, her spine stiffening when she saw the maid standing by an open doorway in which Captain Hulderic lurked.

He bowed and smiled blandly. "You look splendid, Princess."

Rynn ignored him and asked the maid. "Couldn't someone else escort me?"

The maid giggled. "Worry not, Princess. Prince Geraint will meet you in the hall."

Rynn felt a muscle twitch in her eyebrows. "Of course. But someone else, perhaps...?"

"Your fear is unnecessary, Princess," Hulderic said with a polished but false smile. "I will deliver you safely."

Rynn reluctantly stepped into the hallway, glancing over her shoulder when the maid shut the door to her assigned rooms.

"You're doing better than I expected." Hulderic started down the hallway, leaving Rynn to trail after him. "I thought your lack of class would stick out like a sore thumb, but you did well enough greeting the king and queen."

"You don't have to be royalty to have good manners—or *morals*," Rynn said emphatically.

Hulderic chuckled. "Of course, Princess. I'm sure you'll put those good manners on display tonight and play your role. Because if you don't..."

Rynn narrowed her eyes. "What? You'll hold a sword to my neck in front of the whole room?"

She blinked, and in a moment, Hulderic had his hand on her throat and pinned her to the stone wall. "I always thought you would be the most difficult part about Davina's plan," he said pleasantly, even as his fingers dug into her flesh. "No matter. I understand from Davina's spell that you will indeed be forced to say you are her. However, if you don't play your role completely and act as a proper princess, there's no telling what will befall you. Accidents happen, you know. It would be terrible if your life were to end at such a young age."

Rynn felt her blood freeze. She tried to swallow, but Hulderic's grip on her throat made it difficult. *I'm right. There has to be more to this than Davina's escape plan. Why else would he go to such lengths?* Her knees trembled as the depth of Hulderic's threat sank in, and she realized she was in a deadly situation that she only knew the half of. *I need to move carefully. It looks like I really will have to be convincing.*

Hulderic flexed his fingers, applying more pressure on Rynn's throat. "Do you understand?"

Rynn nodded.

Hulderic released her. "Excellent. Come, Princess. Your *fiancé* awaits." Captain Hulderic stalked away, moving down the hallway with the stride of a hungry wolf.

Rynn shivered, then reluctantly followed him. She rubbed her throat and wanted to kick something in her anger and fear. With each minute that passed, the situation seemed to grow increasingly grimmer. *Why did I ever leave home?*

When they reached the hall, Hulderic stepped to the side and bowed with every appearance of respect. "Princess," he murmured.

Rynn ignored him and stepped into the hall—which was a long, rectangular-shaped room lit by glimmering chandeliers and a horse-sized fireplace. One side of the room was made almost entirely of glass, giving a view of Cadburey as the sun set, casting dusty colors and purple shadows across the city.

"Davina—you look lovely!" Prince Geraint smiled as he approached her with the man he had stood by when they first met.

"Thank you." Rynn smiled awkwardly and glanced at Geraint's companion.

Geraint followed her gaze, then smiled. "Ah! Please allow me to introduce you to my dearest friend, Conrad."

His companion bowed and murmured, "Princess." Conrad was taller than the prince by a few inches, and his hair was a darker, ashy shade of brown.

"He is my mother's nephew—my cousin," Geraint added.

Rynn glanced between the two men, taking in the faint family resemblance in their features. "I see. It is an honor to meet you, Conrad."

"The pleasure is mine."

"Conrad works in the government with me," Geraint said.

"Oh? What position do you fill?" Rynn asked.

"All sorts of...roles," Geraint said evasively.

"I hope your journey through Farthendale was pleasant," Conrad asked.

"It mostly was, yes. Though I am very glad to have finally reached Cadburey," Rynn said truthfully. *In spite of Hulderic's threat, I'm not giving up! And my chances of finding help are better here given that my oath forbids me to flee.*

"You look different," Conrad said bluntly.

Rynn blinked. "I beg your pardon?"

"What a jester." Geraint elbowed his cousin and shook his head. "What he meant to say is you don't resemble the portrait your mother sent last year."

"Indeed," Conrad said.

"I agree," Rynn said, mentally scrambling to use the moment to her advantage. "If you compare me to the painting, it's almost as if I'm a *different person*, isn't it?"

Unfortunately, Prince Geraint was too gallant to take the hint. "I don't know anyone who resembles their portrait." He smiled broadly at her. "Tomorrow I shall take you to the royal gallery so you can see my portrait—I look like a dolt."

Rynn let her shoulders drop the smallest bit. "How kind of you to offer."

"What are your thoughts of Farthendale thus far?" Conrad asked.

"Pleasant, I hope!" Geraint added.

"The mountains and forests are very beautiful," Rynn said. "I lived in Torina, which is surrounded by plains with a bit of forest to the northwest—though our woods are nothing like the trees you have here."

Geraint nodded, though Conrad tilted his head slightly and studied Rynn with a thoughtful gaze.

"We're very proud of our forests in Farthendale," Geraint said. "We have some of the oldest—and biggest—woods!"

Rynn tried to discreetly tug on her too-short-sleeve again. "I can't wait to familiarize myself with them."

Conrad cleared his throat and raised his eyebrows at his cousin.

"Right." Geraint stuck his arm out, inviting Rynn to slip her arm in his. "We wanted to ask you about the horse you rode into Cadburey. He's the famed gift horse from the fairies and can talk, yes?"

Rynn reluctantly took his arm. "Falada, yes."

"He is rather beautiful," Conrad said, taking up the space on Rynn's other side.

"Beautiful? He's gorgeous!" Geraint and Conrad led Rynn around the perimeter of the room, smiling (Geraint) and nodding (Conrad) at the lords and ladies who bowed/curtsied. "I don't think I've ever seen a horse that handsome in Farthendale."

"I think it might be his origins," Rynn said. "We have other white horses in Astoria's stables with similar coloring, but none of them glitter as he does. His temperament, however, does not match his appearance. I fear if you were expecting Falada to be a sweet-tempered steed, you will be gravely disappointed."

"He already took a chunk out of the stable holster," Conrad said. "And swore at the stable boys."

"Ahhh yes, that is a fairly accurate sampling of his personality.

I apologize." Rynn winced in sympathy, having been bitten by the horse before. "I do hope the holster isn't in too much pain?"

"No, not at all. He's dealt with worse before...I think," Geraint said.

Rynn tried to smile pleasantly, but when she glanced across the room, she caught sight of a familiar woman: a noble lady with hair as white as milk and deep smile lines. She was also dressed in the long-sleeved, long-skirted gowns of Astoria. *Lady Maela!*

Rynn nibbled on the edge of her lip as she watched the Astorian noblewoman—who had served as the ambassador to Farthendale for years—laugh and chatter with the other guests. Rynn had seen the older lady, who had briefly returned to Astoria to see that the preparations for Princess Davina's upcoming nuptials continued smoothly. *Apparently, things were not as smooth as I had thought. How could she help Davina do this? Perhaps she didn't think she would go through with it? If that is the case, might she help me?*

She opened her mouth to ask Prince Geraint if they could detour over to the Astorian noblewoman, when Lady Maela turned around and set her eyes upon Rynn. "My dear Princess Davina!" Lady Maela exclaimed, crumbling Rynn's hopes.

She swept across the room and embraced Rynn, kissing her on either cheek. "How was your journey? You befell no troubles, I hope?"

"Not exactly..." Rynn said.

Lady Maela arched an eyebrow and nodded—acknowledging the implication. "I imagine it must be a shock to leave your home and everything you've known to come to a new country, but Farthendale is lovely! You will see." Lady Maela patted Rynn's hand consolingly, then turned to the prince and his cousin. "Good evening, Your Highness, Sir Conrad. How dashing you both look this evening!"

Prince Geraint beamed, but Conrad looked back and forth between Rynn and Lady Maela with a furrowed brow.

"Good evening, Lady Maela," Prince Geraint said. "I am glad

you could attend this banquet—I'm sure it does Davina some good to see a familiar face."

"Not that familiar," Rynn muttered under her breath. Though she had seen the lady often—for Lady Maela had privately chatted with Davina a number of times during her visits—as a lady's maid, she was never formally introduced.

"What was that, Davina?" Prince Geraint asked.

Before Rynn could respond, Lady Maela gave Rynn a sympathetic smile. "You must call upon me sometime this week. Though you were prepared for your life here, it is a rather marked difference between being told something and experiencing it. I should love to offer any advice and guidance I can."

Yes! If I can get her alone, I still might be able to convince her this is madness! "I would love that," Rynn said with a little more enthusiasm than was socially acceptable. "How about tomorrow?"

Lady Maela laughed. "You sweet, silly child. I imagine tomorrow you will be rather busy further meeting with your fiancé and his family. But soon, you must visit."

"I *will*," Rynn promised with feeling.

"Good." Lady Maela held the skirt of her dress with one hand and performed a slight curtsey. "Then I shan't take up anymore of your time—this is your first meal in Farthendale, after all. Take care, Your Highness, Your Highness, Sir Conrad!"

"Farewell, Lady Maela," Prince Geraint said cheerfully.

The ambassador was off with a swish of her skirts before Rynn could add anything.

Rynn frowned slightly as she watched Lady Maela approach another guest. *How did Davina convince Lady Maela to help her? She couldn't have paid her off; though she's a princess and could buy whatever she chose, her mother didn't exactly let her slouch around with a pocketful of jewels...*

"A very kind lady," Prince Geraint proclaimed.

"Yes," Rynn said. "I am very glad she is here." She glanced up in time to see Prince Geraint and Conrad exchange glances over her head—no easy task given how tall she was.

"Shall we find our seats?" Conrad prodded after a moment.

"Oh, yes, of course!" Prince Geraint again offered his arm to Rynn. "This way."

The trio fell into awkward silence when they reached the table Rynn assumed they were going to sit at. She curiously glanced from Prince Geraint—who still held her arm—to Conrad—who watched servants whisk past bearing many dishes and bowls.

They're an interesting pair. Geraint is bright smiles and soft eyes. Conrad is less expressive, but he seems calmer, as well.

"You and your soldiers were not the only Astorians to arrive in Cadburey today," Conrad said.

Rynn blinked as his words sank in. *What? Wait, WHAT?!* Could Davina have decided to start her travels in Cadburey? If so, how had Conrad found out?

"Oh?" she asked mildly.

Geraint released Rynn's arm so he could pull back a chair for her. "Ahh, yes, I had forgotten about her."

HER?! A strangled noise squeaked loose from Rynn's throat as she sat down in her chair.

"An Astorian commoner girl was brought in by a wandering minstrel," Geraint continued. "It was remarkable because we so rarely receive travelers—not including merchants or craftsmen—from Astoria, so she was initially brought to the palace as guards assumed she was part of your retinue. She told us she was not, however, and the situation was straightened out."

Rynn had to bite her tongue to keep from shouting over the prince as he relayed the story. "What happened to her?"

Geraint rubbed his chin. "I'm not sure...Conrad, do you remember?" He plopped down in the chair next to Rynn.

Conrad leaned against his chair—which was on Geraint's other side. "She was given work as a goose girl."

Yes! Something has finally worked in my favor! This girl has to be

Davina—she must! Rynn licked her lips. "Then she's still here in Cadburey?"

Geraint nodded.

"She likely will be for a while." Conrad looked out at the swirling masses as the guests began to take their seats. "She was robbed on the road—which is why the minstrel brought her in."

Yep. She didn't last for even a day. Serves her right! When I find her, I'm going to give her a piece of my mind! Rynn couldn't keep the smile off her lips as she said happily, "How frightening that must have been for her."

Conrad furrowed his brow at her, but Geraint leaned forward in his seat. "Yes, I imagine so, but she's safe now." He spared a glance and a warm smile at Rynn. "Don't worry; we will take good care of your previous citizens on your behalf."

Rynn smiled wanly, but Geraint didn't notice—his attention was already back on the nobles.

"Oh—there's Lunette and Arthur—my younger sister and brother." He stood back up and again offered his arm. "Come, we should meet them before we begin."

Rynn stood, her thoughts still focused on Davina. *I'll have to steal away so I can talk to her alone—without hulking Hulderic smiling over my shoulder.*

"Are you coming with us, Conrad?" Geraint asked his cousin.

Conrad shook his head. "No reason to. Hurry back; as soon as your mother arrives, the food will be served." His dark eyes shifted from Geraint to Rynn. He seemed to scrutinize her as his gaze lingered on her face.

Perhaps he would be the one most likely to catch on to my hints? Though it may not be necessary if I can bring Davina around now that she's not an "heiress"...

"Of course," Geraint said sunnily, interrupting Rynn's plotting. "Come, Davina. You're going to love Lunette and Arthur."

IT TOOK two days before it was socially acceptable for Rynn to call upon Lady Maela. Two *long* days.

"Princess Davina!" Lady Maela exclaimed happily when her maid led Rynn into her chambers. "How delighted I am that you have called upon me."

"Yes, thank you." Rynn sat awkwardly on the edge of a cushioned chair.

The maid brought a tea tray over and began pouring as Lady Maela settled into an armchair. "What do you think of Farthendale thus far?"

Rynn opened her mouth to tell the lady *exactly* what she thought of her current situation, but no words leaked out. *Bother —must be the maid. She doesn't know so I can't say anything.* "It's very beautiful," Rynn said. It took everything she had to keep from leaping to her feet and prowling about the room. "And the royal family is very kind."

"They are precious." Lady Maela smiled, making her look grandmotherly.

Rynn blinked. *Precious seems like a slightly condescending word considering how gracious and clever they are...*

The maid finished serving the tea.

"That will be all, Elaine," Lady Maela said to her maid—to Rynn's great relief.

The maid bobbed a curtsy then crept from the sitting room, leaving Rynn alone with the ambassador.

Rynn wasted not a moment. "You must help me reveal the truth."

Lady Maela added a spoonful of sugar to her tea and elegantly stirred it. "And why would I do that?"

"Because this is foolish beyond all reason!" Rynn stood, unable to stay motionless. "Because Davina *needs* to marry Prince Geraint for the good of our countries, and if our deception is uncovered, it will do irreconcilable harm!"

"I agree," Lady Maela said.

Rynn paused. "You do?"

"Yes. Princess Davina—at least whoever the royal family believes is Princess Davina—needs to marry Prince Geraint."

The odd phrasing made Rynn shift uneasily. "Then you'll speak for me?"

"No." Lady Maela sipped her tea.

"But you just said—!" Rynn broke off her sentence and forced herself to relax her shoulders and sit down. *Yelling at a noble lady isn't likely to impress her. I need to be calm—though I would dearly love to chuck a teacup at the wall.*

Lady Maela smiled and set her teacup down. "The question you need to ask is *why* did I agree to help Davina."

Rynn hesitated. "I rather assumed you thought Davina wouldn't go through with her plan."

"Not at all," Lady Maela said. "It was I who recommended Captain Hulderic and his men and suggested to Davina that she compel you to take her place."

Rynn's jaw nearly unhinged. "But if you helped her...that's practically treason."

Lady Maela swatted her hand through the air. "Nonsense! Before I offered to help her, the fool girl nearly killed herself trying to climb from her tower bedroom."

Rynn blinked. "What?" *I did not think Davina had that much gumption.*

"Queen Cassia covered it up. I only knew of it because I was with the queen when a guard came to tell her. But it became quite clear that Davina would take drastic measures to avoid her future, no matter how her mother ignored it. So I helped her."

"But *why?*"

"Because I would much rather have a lady's maid on the throne of Farthendale than a day-dreaming girl who isn't much use to anyone," Lady Maela said.

Rynn pulled back at the statement, unsettled. *It is true that*

Davina has driven me mad with her imaginings, but to say she is of no use?

"I can see you disapprove, but Queen Cassia agrees with me." Lady Maela sipped her tea again. "Davina is the eldest daughter in the royal family. By all rights, she should rule, yes?"

Rynn nodded slowly.

"Unfortunately, she is irresponsible and immature. She would drive Astoria into the ground within months after being crowned. Marrying Davina to Prince Geraint is the only respectable way the queen was able to dump her off and remove her from the line of succession, freeing Prince Casimir or Prince Bernhard to inherit the throne. Of course, sending her to Farthendale was a double boon, as it also gave her a chance to strengthen our uneasy relationship."

Lady Maela set her teacup down with a quiet clack. "Queen Cassia, however, did not properly consider her daughter's selfishness. Davina is determined to do what she wishes. She may no longer be in line for the crown of Astoria, but she could still ruin the country by fouling up her marriage. Helping Davina plan so there at least was a substitute was the best outcome I could foresee."

Rynn chewed on her lip as she thought.

"Cheer up," Lady Maela said. "Your situation has vastly improved. You will have luxury beyond your imagination, and you'll certainly make a better queen than Davina."

"I think you are selling her short," Rynn said. "It's true, she's silly and self-centered, but you haven't given her the chance to prove herself."

Lady Maela frowned slightly, and Rynn shrugged. "It is a possibility, anyway," she added lamely. *I am not feeling particularly charitable to Davina at the moment. In fact, I would happily wish Falada upon her! But this portrait of her does seem overly harsh.*

"Who are your parents, girl?" the noblewoman asked.

It took a moment for Rynn to calculate her reply. "John and

Martha—they are merchants in Torina," Rynn said, naming the capital of Astoria.

Lady Maela slowly nodded. "I see." She peered at her teacup. "In any case, I can understand your anxiety, but allow me to assure you that I shall be your ally in this. No Astorians who visit the palace shall decry you."

Rynn relaxed, but not because of Lady Maela's vow of help—particularly given it was the *wrong* kind of help!

It was more that Rynn's family was slightly odd—and not just because she was one of seven children. Her parents were originally poor woodcutters before her father saved an elderly woman and her granddaughter from a wolf. Somehow the Fairy Council had gotten word of her father's good deed, and sent a fairy godfather to reward them.

The fairy godfather set them up in Torina as wealthy merchants. The way her parents told the story, they bemoaned this fate and often sighed over the abrupt change in their life even though they had more riches than they ever could have hoped to achieve, and went on to have a boisterous and prosperous family.

Rynn privately thought her parents were over-romanticizing their life as woodcutters, and it irked her that they seemed to cling to their old memories—for though they had no need to, they kept poultry and cows at their city home.

Even so, she was always reluctant to share her family's history. For the fairy godfather still occasionally mucked with their lives, and it wasn't often that folk seemed to properly grasp the quixotic nature of magic.

In fact, in most cases, it seemed to Rynn that those for whom magic managed to work pleasantly (namely her parents) didn't accept it, and to those that magic seemed more of a curse (the royal Astorian family and their blind insistence that Falada was a magnificent blessing) were oblivious.

"You will accept your new role?" Lady Maela asked, jarring Rynn from her thoughts.

Rynn pressed her lips together.

"I will not help you reverse this, child," Lady Maela said gently. "I think in time you will see why. Besides, you haven't much of a choice. Davina is gone," Lady Maela said.

Rynn opened her mouth, intending to tell the noblewoman that the princess was very likely in Cadburey, but the words died in her throat before she uttered more than a squeak. *Perhaps I shouldn't tell her. She is so set against Davina that she might approach her and drive the princess away. Convincing Davina to come forward very well might be my last chance to fix this.*

"Thank you for your frankness, Lady Maela," Rynn said, tactfully switching topics.

Lady Maela smiled. "Of course. If you ever need any advice in your new life, do not hesitate to seek me out."

"You are very kind." Rynn smiled as pleasantly as she could, though inwardly, her heart beat with rebellion. *Fine. Lady Maela may be a dead end, but there is hope. Davina's difficulties may make her more willing to return! I must confirm the new goose girl is her.*

CHAPTER 3
UNEXPECTED ALLIES

Another day passed before Rynn was able to steal her way down to the stables under the pretext of wanting to see Falada to hide her real mission: finding Davina. (It had taken her ten minutes to convince her maid it was not necessary to call for a guard escort. The *last* thing she needed was for Hulderic to catch wind of her activities!)

It took Rynn the better part of an hour before she found the stables, mostly because the building was so ornate and almost fortress-like, she walked past it twice without recognizing it. It wasn't until a footman pointed at it that she discovered what it really was.

The "stable" was three stories tall. The bottom was comprised of the horse stalls; the top floor served as hay/grain storage; and the middle floor housed an army of blacksmiths, saddlers, and an herbwoman who daily sprinkled the stalls with sweet-smelling herbs. The stable even sported a wooden tower!

Rynn squinted in the fierce sunlight and shook her head. "Farthendale must really treasure their horses." She reluctantly approached the building, finally hearing the sounds of horses nickering and calling to one another.

When she ventured through the doors, a stablehand almost collapsed at her feet.

"Thank goodness you've come, Princess!" He rubbed a bruise on his bare forearm and shivered.

"Um," Rynn eloquently said.

"Your horse has been...missing you," he continued.

"I doubt that," she muttered.

"Come, I will show you to him and get him saddled." The stablehand marched down the aisle with great resolution.

"Er, I actually only wanted to take a peek at him to make sure he's fine." Rynn followed in the stablehand's wake, trying to figure out how to regain control of the situation. "Maybe exchange a few words of pleasantries—or curses on his end."

"He needs to be exercised," the stablehand said firmly.

Oh, bells of hades, NO. I only came here to throw Hulderic off track if he asked where I went this morning. I need to find out where the geese are. I am not riding that nightmare! "You could just set him loose," Rynn suggested.

The stablehand bulged his eyes and shook his head. "Can't risk it, Princess. Who knows what evil the beast will do if freed!"

"You have a point," Rynn admitted.

The stablehand stopped in front of a fine stall that smelled of pine and had a horse carved into the door. A glittering, snow-white butt was visible just behind the door.

"Hello, Falada," Rynn said.

Falada turned slightly so he could sneer at her, then kicked out with a hind foot and smacked the wooden door with a loud crack.

"I'll go fetch your saddle," the stablehand said.

"Wait," Rynn called, but he ran off before she could protest further.

"What do you want?" Falada asked.

Rynn sighed and pushed a lock of her amber hair out of her face. "The stablehand thinks you need to be ridden."

Falada snorted.

"That's what I said," Rynn agreed.

Falada snagged a chunk of hay and chewed it, narrowing his eyes—which were as black as his soul. "Why are you here?"

"I said the stablehand—"

"Would not have presumed to summon a princess over a bothersome horse."

Rynn paused, then shrugged. *What harm is there in telling him the truth?* "I want to find out where the geese are being kept."

"So you came to the *stables*?"

"I'm trying to avoid drawing attention to myself."

Falada selected another mouthful of hay. "You don't wish for the wolf masquerading as a soldier to find out?"

Rynn nodded reluctantly. *He is unfortunately observant. I hope he doesn't decide to tell Hulderic out of sheer spite.*

"Very well." Falada's voice was gravelly and rough. "The geese are taken into a meadow during the day. Find out where it is, then agree to ride me. I will take you there."

Rynn tilted her chin up and narrowed her eyes. "Why should I trust you? I know what you're capable of."

"Because if I have to spend another moment next to a good-natured mushroom, I will go mad," Falada said flatly.

Rynn peered up and down the aisle, wondering what he meant. When the fairy horse nodded to the stalls on either side of him, Rynn peered into them. Though much of the stable was devoted to very fine horses, the stalls immediately surrounding Falada all housed short, fat ponies that ranged in colors from gray to an earthy brown.

If Falada had been anyone else, Rynn would have laughed at the description, but she didn't dare anger the horse.

"Alright," she agreed, just as the stablehand returned, carrying a gold-leafed bridle and saddle.

The stablehand paused with his hand on the door latch to Falada's stall and shivered.

Taking pity on the man—and perhaps feeling dangerously daring after her talk with Falada—Rynn cleared her throat. "You'll let this nice stablehand get you saddled without harming him. Won't you, Falada?"

Falada bared his teeth at her, then gave the stablehand a withering glare. "Fine."

The stablehand almost fainted with relief, but he scrambled into the stall and hurriedly saddled Falada. He was so pre-occupied, he didn't seem to notice Rynn's discreet questions as she slowly wheedled the location of the goose meadow from him.

Only a few short minutes later, Rynn found herself unceremoniously thrown into Falada's saddle and set free just outside the barn.

"You heard his directions?" Rynn asked.

Falada flicked his white tail and pawed at the dirt. "Yes."

"Great. There's just one problem: I don't know how to leave Cadburey except to go through the front entrance, which seems like a spectacular waste of time."

Falada started walking. "There are several entrances around the palace so the servants can take the livestock—and horses—out to graze."

"You've seen them?"

"They sent me out to pasture with the mushrooms."

Rynn cleared her throat. *Don't laugh. Don't! He won't take it well.* "I see."

Falada sidled around the stables. Wherever he went, a pathway among the people opened up like magic.

"It's been less than a week, and already your reputation proceeds you," Rynn muttered.

Falada snorted. "I'd be upset if it didn't."

Rynn grinned wryly and gave Falada more slack in the reins as he stalked towards a large wooden door built into the wall that surrounded the castle.

Two soldiers scrambled to open it, and within moments, Rynn and Falada were free of the palace.

Cadburey was situated on top of a hill, so Falada had to pick his way down it. But the areas behind the palace opened up into lush, green meadows that had been cleared for livestock. Mountains loomed on the skyline in the distance, and beyond the meadows was a sea of trees.

Creamy brown cows mooed as they grazed at the bottom of the hill, and the jingle of the goats' collar bells chimed in the background, creating a song as the goats jumped around on the hill.

Falada ignored these animals and turned to continue around the backside of the palace. "Hold on," he said tersely.

Rynn clung to the saddle as Falada rocked into a smooth, but *fast*, ground-covering canter.

The fairy horse tossed his head, but—true to his word—refrained from any movements that would dislodge Rynn from his back.

Her hair sweeping behind her and the mountains stretching before her, Rynn almost *enjoyed* the ride. (Or she would have, if she still hadn't thought Falada might attempt to unexpectedly dump her.)

They followed the slope of the hill for several minutes before Rynn spotted the white dots that marked the geese. Two people—a lad and a young lady with the same sunshine blonde hair as Davina—were perched on boulders positioned by a small river.

It's her—it must be! Rynn grinned as Falada bore down on the pair, slowing to a walk when they were a stone's throw from them.

Rynn's heart sang when she saw that the new goose girl was indeed Davina. The princess waved to Rynn but did not leave her boulder as she combed out her long hair. "Hello, Princess Davina!" the real Davina called.

Rynn narrowed her eyes at the princess, then glanced at her companion. The goose boy was about ten years old and wore a green beret that was at least two sizes too big for his head; it almost drooped over his eyes. He squinted at her, looking from Davina to Rynn.

Falada tossed his head again when Rynn slipped off the saddle and landed on the ground. Falada was taller than most horses, so the landing jarred her bones.

Rynn hurriedly backed away from him to get out of biting range. "I need to talk to...her. If you run loose, will you promise not to trample the geese?"

Falada shifted his gaze to Davina. For a moment, Rynn hoped he would say something, but he only blew out of his nostrils with enough force to make Davina flinch before he turned his butt to her. "Call when you are ready to leave." He trotted off, the stirrups of the saddle slapping his sides and the reins dangling over his neck.

Rynn hurried up to Davina, her mouth opening and closing as the stupid oath kept her from uttering Davina's name. *If I can't say her name, what am I supposed to call her?*

Davina must have guessed the problem, for she pushed the luxurious curtain of her hair over her shoulders and opened her arms wide. "Yes, Princess, it is I. Vina!"

Rynn paused mid-step and stared at the princess. *She can't be serious. Is she really that dim-witted?* Judging by the way Davina smiled proudly at her new alias, she was. *No matter, that might help me reveal the truth!*

"Vina, I am so glad to see you are safe." Rynn took Davina's hand and squeezed it.

"Indeed, I am doing quite well, if I say so myself! Please allow me to introduce you to my associate." Davina elegantly flicked her long fingers in the goose boy's direction. "This is Little Conrad, my fellow goose keeper."

Rynn blinked. *Conrad? Must be a common name.* Rynn smiled at the boy. "Hello, Conrad."

"*Little* Conrad," Davina stressed.

Little Conrad chewed the stem of a blade of grass and nodded. "Hallo," he said.

Though Davina smiled benevolently at him, Rynn returned her attention to the princess. "What happened to you? I thought you had...other plans."

"Indeed, but they were ruined not an hour after I left you." Davina sighed and placed a hand over her heart as the blue of her eyes turned mournful. "I was *robbed*! It was frightening! The cutthroats took everything—my horse, coin, and provisions. I was left with nothing but the dress on my back! It was positively *shocking*!"

"I don't doubt it was a terrifying experience." Rynn tipped her head as she inspected the princess from head to foot and was relieved to see no visible injuries. "But why shocking?"

"I can't believe they took *everything*!" Davina shook her head as wildly as Falada would.

Rynn blinked. "You were an unescorted, unsupervised young lady traveling through a forest. It's surprising they let you *go*! Did they hurt you?"

"No, no, no." Davina repositioned herself on her boulder and placed her hands in her lap. "But that they would take everything from me—an unarmed lady as you said—is shocking. I have heard the ballads of highway men, and they never harm young ladies! If they do steal from them, it is only a handful of jewels and a kiss—though I still might have objected to *that* for they were not handsome as the ballads promised. The ruffians didn't even have all their teeth!"

Rynn inhaled deeply and rubbed her temple. *It's not her fault she doesn't understand the harsh realities of this world...but can she really be* that *oblivious?* "Vina, thieves, highway men, and cutthroats steal from everyone. That's why they're *called* thieves, highway men, and cutthroats!"

"Well, I know that now!" Davina rolled her eyes.

I better change the topic before I am tempted to take her by the shoulders and shake her. Rynn forced her shoulders to ease and watched Falada graze in the pasture. "If you were robbed, how did you end up in Cadburey?"

Davina's eyes shone as she clasped her hands beneath her chin. "Oh! It was the most delightful thing! A wandering minstrel found me and walked me to Cadburey—he even let me ride his donkey! He was such a sight, dressed in all blue and strumming a lyre as his bell-covered donkey trotted next to him! He made certain I wasn't injured, then he brought me all the way to the palace! Isn't that honorable?"

"It is," Rynn agreed, watching a goose approach Falada. The fairy horse snapped at it, but instead of retreating, the goose smacked him in the sneering face with his white wings, honked, then waddled off in victory. Rynn smiled at the display, until Davina spoke again and grabbed every bit of Rynn's attention.

"Which is why I have decided to give up on my dream," she announced.

Rynn perked as the world brightened. "Oh? You'll return to your proper place?"

Davina rolled her eyes. "No, silly. I'm going to be a wandering minstrel!"

Rynn lowered her brows as she puzzled over Davina's words. "A wandering minstrel?"

"Yes! I just have to save up enough money for a lyre so I can begin to earn my keep. I am a talented singer—Mama always told me so—but to be a real minstrel, I must have an instrument as well."

Rynn was somewhat gratified when Little Conrad—still sitting on his rock—eyed Davina as if she were mad. *At least I'm not the only one who questions her plans.* "Why a wandering minstrel?"

"Because it will be so *romantic*, don't you think? Ambling from town to town, singing for my bread and a roof over my head..."

Davina sighed blissfully, then got to braiding her hair. "Lyres aren't even that expensive, you know. Or at least they wouldn't be, if King Othmar wasn't so *cheap*! He barely pays his servants any wage at all! Did you know that?"

"I imagine it is because he is also paying for your housing and food? That was the common practice *your mother* adopted as well," Rynn said.

Davina stuck her nose up in the air. "Regardless! With such stingy wages, it will be weeks afore I can afford a lyre. Unless..." She smiled gamely at Rynn.

"I am *not* giving you money for a lyre," Rynn said flatly. "You need to give up on your ridiculous dreams and reclaim your birthright!"

Davina pressed her lips together and looked away from her. "Don't you want me to be happy?"

"I want you to do what is *right*!" Rynn massaged the back of her neck in her frustration and glanced at Little Conrad.

The lad seemed more intent on watching the frogs that jumped in the stream than their conversation. *If only he was Prince Geraint, or an adult. While our conversation might not be enough to tip anyone off on Davina's real identity, it would certainly raise suspicions! I can't believe she is being this stubborn. I would have thought the robbers would have been enough to make her regret her decision.* Rynn eyed Davina with a tiny sliver of respect. *It seems she has more iron in her will than I gave her credit for.*

Falada swore loudly, and Rynn swiveled in time to see a goose yank on his tail and run off. Falada was on the miscreant goose in a second, his teeth closing over the animal's neck.

Her heart in her throat, Rynn shouted, "Falada!"

The horse froze for a moment or two before releasing the goose—though he did snort at it and yank a tailfeather from the goose's white behind.

Rynn relaxed again, relieved. *I can't imagine the king will react well if he is told the princess's fairy horse killed one of his geese.*

A small frown crossed Davina's lips. "He listened to you."

"Only because it suited him," Rynn said. "He hates the stables, and he promised to be good if I took him out."

"He hated the stables back in Torina, too," Davina said.

Rynn shrugged her shoulders. "He's Falada. He probably hates everywhere." Davina did not look convinced, but Rynn ignored her and plowed ahead. "I assume this means you'll remain employed as a goose girl for the foreseeable future?"

Davina once again tilted her chin up. "Since you will not help me, yes."

"Good." Rynn said. It occurred to her that Lady Maela may very well be willing to give the princess the funds for a lyre, simply to be rid of her. *Yes, it's best if they don't meet.*

She pulled on the skirts of her dress—the princess's dress—which flashed an inch of her ankle thanks to her taller frame.

Davina pursed her lips. "That looks a little tight on you."

Rynn snorted. "That's not my fault, is it?"

Davina shook her head as if she were a wise old woman. "You would be much happier if you learned to be content in your circumstances."

The urge to shake Davina made Rynn's fingers twitch. "I hope you know that applies to *you* as well."

"Of course! That's why even though the king horribly underpays his people, I am still happy!" Davina smiled brightly.

Rynn felt tired just looking at her. *Six younger siblings—though Eva doesn't count—but I met my match of wills in a day-dreamer princess who can barely keep herself alive.* "I have to go."

"Very well, Princess. Thank you for stopping to see me!" Davina declared from the throne of her boulder.

"Mmhmm. I'll be back," Rynn warned. When she noticed Little Conrad was watching her, she waved to him. "It was nice to meet you."

He pushed his cap up and squinted at Rynn—apparently wondering if she, too, was mad.

I don't blame him, Rynn thought as she waded through the grass and made her way to the grazing Falada. *This all feels like a mad dream.*

CHAPTER 4
THE FAIRY GODFATHER

Rynn pondered Davina's stubborn decision and Lady Maela's biased beliefs well into the following day. She spent her spare moments trying to figure out how to oust herself or convince Davina to reclaim her title.

The situation grows increasingly dire with every passing hour, Rynn thought grimly to herself as she shifted her wine goblet and tried not to fidget. *The longer we run with this farce, the greater the chance will be that King Othmar and Queen Morgaine will* not *forgive us.* She glanced around the table, her eyes seeking out the king and queen at the far end.

Geraint—who sat across from her—smiled when she met his gaze. Conrad—Rynn's only other companion since Prince Arthur, who had been at her other side, had retired earlier with Princess Lunette—glanced at her cup.

"Do you need more refreshment?" Conrad asked.

"No, thank you. I am quite fine." Rynn cleared her throat awkwardly and wished for the din and background hum banquets typically provided to cover the silence.

Since the first night of her arrival, the royal family had taken the majority of their dinners as family meals. Besides the royal family, often the king's or queen's siblings would join them, as well as a number of their children. Tonight, the only other family members present were Conrad and his father—Lord Medrod, the Queen's brother.

Lord Medrod, who served as an advisor to King Othmar—though as far as Rynn could tell, they were mostly just close friends—leaned back in his chair and tapped his fingers on the gleaming table surface. "I received word today: Astoria means to impose another tax on all wood imports."

"Again?" King Othmar sighed. "They persist in tightening the noose."

"You could increase the export tax on precious metals," Queen Morgain suggested.

"No, you can't push them too much with the price of metals and gems, or they'll start mining their mountains in the north out of desperation," Lord Medrod said.

Farthendale, thanks to its ore-rich mountains, was the major provider of metals and gems for Astoria's craftsmen, but Rynn suspected Medrod was right. Astoria hadn't tapped its side of the mountain range that partially divided the two countries because it hadn't yet been worth the trouble.

But if they raise the price high enough, it will suddenly become very much worth it. Rynn considered a bowl of salted nuts—since arriving in Farthendale, she had found both nuts and mushrooms had become a staple of her diet—and tried to avoid calling attention to herself.

"No, just increase the export tax on paper," Lord Medrod continued. "Those flat-footed plainsmen can't seem to get enough of the stuff. They must line their walls with it."

The suggestion made Rynn cringe. *We don't line our walls, we write* books! *Then again, I shouldn't expect them to understand. The Farthendale royal library is abysmal.* She had seen it on her tour and had been *most* disappointed. Ellie—one of Rynn's sisters who had a passion for books and studying—would have been horrified if she ever saw it.

Conrad shifted next to Rynn. "You disagree, Princess?"

Rynn bit her tongue to keep from cursing her luck that the eagle-eyed Conrad had noticed her reaction. "It is merely that Astorians treasure books and learning. It's why Astoria much admires the country of Anura and its private library. Taxing paper will make many Astorians...disappointed."

"Ahhh, yes. I had nearly forgotten we have an Astorian princess in our midst who can explain the strange musings of her country and her mother." Lord Medrod raised his wine cup to her, looking down his hawkish nose—one of his resemblances to his sister—at her.

"Brother." Queen Morgain's voice held a note of warning. "Davina will soon be my daughter-in-law. You *will* treat her with kindness and respect."

Lord Medrod sighed. "I know, I know. Sorry, Davina. It is merely that sometimes we so absolutely do *not* understand your people." He shook his head. "We see passive-aggressive advances and abuses where, likely, your people have no idea the insult was given. Even with Lady Maela around, she hasn't been able to bridge the gap between us."

Rynn bowed her head. "I understand that our cultures—and countries—value different things, Lord Medrod."

Conrad studied his fork. "Fancy that, Father. A young princess is more understanding than you—an adult and an advisor to the king."

While the others chuckled amidst Medrod's protests, Rynn furrowed her brow and studied Conrad. *He and Geraint must be very good friends if he's willing to risk his father's wrath to lighten the moment. Or is he just that politically motivated?*

Conrad looked up and, upon meeting Rynn's gaze, bowed his head to her.

Rynn studied his dark, bottomless eyes. ...*No...I don't think he did that out of any ulterior motive.*

King Othmar interrupted Rynn's thoughts. "This just shows that it will be good for us to welcome a royal Astorian into our family. I am glad, Davina, you are here."

The king smiled handsomely, making Rynn's heart twist. *They are so kind, and their trust is so terribly misplaced in me.* Rynn smiled wanly at the king and was relieved when he returned his attention to Sir Medrod.

"Father, it is growing late. May we not be excused? Conrad and I have work to discuss, and surely Davina does not wish to spend her evening at this table," Prince Geraint said.

King Othmar waved a hand at him. "Of course. Good evening, you three."

"Good evening," Rynn and the cousins chorused.

Rynn took Geraint's arm, though he spoke mostly with Conrad and paid her little attention as he led her all the way back to her rooms.

"Yes, we'll have to buy another shipment of dyes from Caldonia," Geraint said.

"Indeed," Conrad said. "Which will provide another reason to approach your father about the repairs the harbor cities need after that last storm."

He seems so well informed about everything. I wonder what his official role really is. Will he take over after his father and advise Geraint?

Rynn risked glancing at Conrad and felt slightly embarrassed to find his eyes fixed on her, his expression unreadable. Rynn hurriedly looked away, then glanced at him again when she thought he would have looked away. He hadn't.

Still scrutinizing her, Conrad tilted his head. "You should wish the princess good night."

Geraint blinked then looked from Conrad to Rynn. "Why?"

Rynn kept her attention on Geraint—who felt much safer with his easy smiles than Conrad did with his dark, observant gaze—and smiled lightly. "Perhaps because we have stopped outside my rooms?"

"Oh. Oh!" Geraint laughed sheepishly. "I do apologize, Davina. You must think my mother raised me in a barn. Sleep well —I look forward to seeing you in the morning. Mother wishes to spend the morning discussing wedding plans."

Rynn's smile froze. "I shall look forward to it. Good night, Prince Geraint, Conrad." She curtsied, then slipped into her room before Geraint could say anything more.

Once inside the room, her smile fell from her lips like a lead weight, and she leaned against the wooden door. *Thank you, Geraint, for that additional reminder that time is running out.* Rynn shivered as she heard their voices retreat down the hallway. A few moments passed before she pushed off the door and began pacing the length of her room.

"I knew our countries' relationship was strained, but I did not properly take into account how very *tense* the situation is. Davina, you thoughtless girl! You're going to ruin Astoria's relationship with Farthendale because you want to *sing*!" Rynn plucked a pillow from her bed and threw it at the door. "And it is beyond me how Lady Maela can pretend this will not end in a tragedy!"

She breathed heavily and glared at the pillow, thankful for the chance to vent some of her frustration. A moment passed before she plopped face-first on the bed. "This can't be happening to me," she moaned. "It's a nightmare! It's not like I can just give in and be the princess—there *will* be other visitors from Astoria who will know I am not Davina! But Davina's so *thick-headed*, who knows if I'll ever get through to her, and Lady Maela isn't likely to believe in Davina unless she does something intelligent for once!"

Rynn pushed herself into a sitting position on her bed and tried to think. *Perhaps there is a way. Davina wanted to be a minstrel after one saved her...could I arrange for her to meet Geraint? He's handsome and kind; she just might fall in love with him as easily as she fell in love with a bad career choice! But how can I lure him out to the goose meadow?*

Rynn sighed and flopped back down on her bed. "If I had someone, anyone to discuss this with, it might be easier." She curled her fingers into fists, trying to battle off the loneliness that threatened to overtake her. *I'd give anything to talk to Eva—or any of my siblings! Someone who knows the real me...*

"I could always summon Mortimer," Rynn muttered.

Mortimer was the fairy godfather who had rewarded Rynn's parents for their good deed. As he had continued to pop in on the family even after rewarding her parents—mostly because he had to fill his quota of wish fulfillments and needed a new target—he had given the family a somewhat humiliating phrase they could repeat to summon him.

Rynn had never done so. Her fondness and respect for the fairy godfather had plummeted after he had "blessed" (or more correctly cursed) Eva with magical powers.

She picked at the coverlet on her bed. "Maybe it's time to change that..."

Mortimer might, after all, be able to break the vow Davina had forced on her. *Yes! If he can rid me of that stupid vow, I can fix this all myself!*

Rynn abruptly sat up again and crawled off the edge of the bed. *What was that awful phrase we're supposed to use again?* She strained her memory. "I think it was: *Oh, great fairy godfather Mortimer! I, a stupid human, humbly need your magnificent and wonderful magic!*"

An eruption of light and a loud bang—like a tea kettle exploding—filled the room. Rynn took a step back and tried to blink the stars out of her eyes.

"WHO DARED TO SUMMON ME IN THE MIDDLE OF MY RESEARCH?" a deep voice shouted with such volume, Rynn felt it in her stomach. "SOPHIA, IF YOU—oh. It's you, the oldest brat."

When Rynn's eyesight finally cleared, she found Mortimer, his arms folded—making his gray robes strain in the shoulders—and his hooded blue eyes narrowed.

He was a rather unlikely fairy. His skin was not smooth and baby soft, but instead he perpetually bore facial stubble and furrowed brows. His grayish hair always looked as if he ran his hands through it and yanked on it, and his fairy wings—transparent and sparkly—were markedly *smaller* than the average fairy's.

"What do you want?" Mortimer barked. "I'm busy with my research, and if you ruined my experiment by summoning me for something entirely unnecessary, I will see that you live to regret it."

Even though I could tell Mortimer everything as he's a fairy, not a human, so my vow won't apply to him, it won't do to tell the whole story. He'll get bored and wander off without helping me. Rynn licked her lips and mentally condensed her request into the shortest phrasing possible. "A thoughtless young lady used a fairy handkerchief to compel me into a vow of silence so I can't tell the truth about a certain matter. I wish for you to break the vow so I can speak freely."

"Can't be done," Mortimer said without hesitation.

"It can't be done, or you won't do it?" Rynn asked.

Mortimer eyed her, making his already bunched brow wrinkle further. "It's unfortunate you have a shred more intelligence than your ungrateful parents. Fine. It *can* be done, but I'm not going to do it. Do you have any idea how much work it would require? And all the reports I'd have to submit to the fairy council—for *you*? My talents are far better used focusing on my research."

Rynn spoke through clenched jaws. "Then what good is a fairy godfather who won't save his godchild?"

"Testy, aren't you? If you took a moment to think, you'll realize I didn't say I *wouldn't* help you." Mortimer waggled a long finger in Rynn's face. "As it just so happens, you are in luck. I am a wish short of my quota for the month, so I will fix the mess you've gotten yourself into."

Rynn grabbed a post of her canopy bed and scooted around the mattress. "No, no. It's fine. I can handle it."

"You're a human," Mortimer scoffed. "You can barely handle staying alive. You said you wanted to be able to speak freely and tell the truth—so I'll do you one better. I'll make you so charismatic you can get people to do whatever you want."

"*No*." Rynn retreated behind her bed and shook her head. *I was an idiot for calling him! If he gives me a magical gift, it'll make everything worse! Eva's still suffering from the last wish he fulfilled for her!* "No, I have no need of magical powers! It's fine. I apologize for interrupting your research, but if you aren't powerful enough to break my vow, I'll manage alone."

"So now you *insult* me? Listen up, my pea-brained godchild, once this gift settles on you, you'll be so thankful, you'll want to kiss my shoes. For now, I grant you the ability of charisma so powerful even the very air listens to you!"

Mortimer jabbed a finger at Rynn again, and a gust of magic swirled through her bedroom with such force, it almost ripped the canopy off its frame and put out the small fire that crackled in the fireplace.

The wind circled Rynn, yanking on her hair and clothes as it wound tighter and tighter around her. Her tongue burned as if she had just drunk scalding soup, and just as abruptly as it arrived, the wind died off.

Rynn pushed her amber hair out of her face. "That was *not* charisma!"

"You are right," Mortimer said. "I thought it would be more interesting if I played with the phrasing a bit. Congratulations, you can now control the wind."

Rynn gaped at the fairy—her hair and dress still unkempt—and tried to summon any sort of emotion besides shock.

"You may commence with the kissing of my shoes whenever you like." Mortimer stuck a foot out and waited expectantly.

"Are you *crazy*?" Rynn shouted. "Wind control is the last gift I need! I'm posing as Princess Davina while staying in *Farthendale*! How do you think Prince Geraint will react when he finds out his fiancée has obtained magical powers overnight?"

Mortimer squinted. "Farthendale? No wonder it seemed extra stuffy for the human world. There's not much magic here."

"*Exactly*," Rynn spat. She winced when the vehemence of her words made one of the canopy curtains flutter with her new magic. "Farthendale doesn't see much magic *ever*. They won't react happily when they learn what has happened."

Mortimer shrugged. "Don't tell them. Problem solved."

"It's an additional problem I can't deal with on top of the role of playing fake princess," Rynn said.

"Well you should have thought about that before asking for my help."

"I asked you to nullify a vow, not give me magical powers!" Again, a wind flared with Rynn's anger, though this time it slammed into the fairy godfather, who brushed it off with ease.

He rolled his eyes. "Ungrateful, just like your parents. Obviously, you can do *so much better* on your own. I will leave you to your little drama."

"Wait, take the powers back." Rynn took a few hurried steps closer to Mortimer.

"I think not," Mortimer said. "Since you know *everything*, you can handle a bit of magic. Maybe it will teach you to be more thankful."

Rynn gasped a little—which seemed to suck the air from the room and made it a little harder to breathe for a moment. She coughed, then shook her head. "Please!"

"Your pretty manners are too late. Now don't bother me again!" Mortimer straightened the collar of his robe and was gone with another flash of light.

Rynn stared at his vacated spot for several long moments before her legs gave out, and she plopped down on the floor in a heap. *That didn't make things better...it's far worse now!* She pressed her hands to her mouth to keep herself from crying and shook her head.

What do I do now? What can I do? The hopelessness of the situation finally broke past her control, and tears spilled down Rynn's cheeks as she leaned against her bed, and a breeze snapped the skirts of her dress.

THE FOLLOWING DAY, Rynn, exhausted and fatigued thanks to her sleepless night, sagged for a moment on Falada's back as the white horse walked across the meadow. He made for the boulder where Davina was splayed, once again combing her golden hair as her goose charges roamed the meadow.

Why is it that I suffer greatly for the short bout of stupidity I had in thinking Mortimer would help, but Princess Davina—who launched the most insipidly senseless plan ever—gets to wile her days away combing her hair and sunning herself?

Rynn had spent the entirety of the night trying to grasp the mechanics of her newly bequeathed powers. They weren't as wild as she had initially feared and were tied to her words—as Mortimer had outlined when he foisted them upon her. While her control was still shaky at best, if Rynn kept her mouth shut, they did not stir.

Additionally, Rynn had learned that the power of the winds appeared to be tied to the strength at which she spoke. And, if she spoke directly to the wind, it would do her bidding. Otherwise, it did whatever it wanted.

It's a more rebellious power than I would have liked, but as long as I make sure I have the expressiveness of a rock, I can manage. Once this mess is over, I will call Mortimer and demand *he take the powers back.*

Though, if I am lucky, they might fade on their own...he did say he granted me these powers "for now."

Falada stopped next to the small stream near Davina's rock, and Rynn blinked her bleary eyes. "Thank you, Falada." She slipped off his back and nearly fell down when she landed on the ground.

Falada chewed on his bit and turned his head so he could roll his eyes at her. "Are you ill?"

Rynn shook her head to clear it and forced her shoulders back. "I'm fine, thank you." She patted his shoulder and zipped away when she heard the horse chew louder. Massaging the back of her neck, Rynn meandered towards Davina, offering Little Conrad a wan smile when he bowed to her.

Squinting in the sharp sunlight, Rynn tried to push the pounding headache from her mind. "Vina. You have to come forward and tell the truth."

Davina huffed and set her comb aside. "How foolish of me. Here I had thought you were coming to visit me or give me the money I deserve, but instead you came only to browbeat me into what *you* perceive as being right."

"This has nothing to do with *my* beliefs or perceptions, Vina. This *will* end poorly." Rynn was glad she was tired; it made it easier to keep her voice expressionless so she didn't yell at the princess and loosen a gale upon her.

Davina scrambled off her rock. "I don't have to listen to this. In fact, I *won't*! Just because you care more about the country than me doesn't give you a right to scold me."

Rynn trailed her as the princess stomped across the meadow, following the stream. "Do you hear yourself? Do you really think you should be allowed to put yourself ahead of the good of your country—your *people*?"

Davina sniffed. "You are such a hypocrite. You harp all day long, and yet you refuse to sacrifice *yourself* for the country."

"That's not a fair comparison." Rynn felt her eyebrow twitch in anger. "It's *because* I'm worried for our country that I'm thinking ahead to what will happen when—not if—we are found out."

"I don't believe you." Davina patted the head of a goose who ignored her and plucked at the lush meadow grass.

"I'm *not* being selfish." Rynn clenched her jaw to keep her frustration in. (How could Davina declare they were the same, when Rynn was plagued with magic and was on the way to being executed for impersonating a royal!)

Davina turned around and placed her hands on her hips. "Oh? Then what *are* you doing?"

"I'M TRYING TO KEEP US ALIVE!"

Wind ripped through the meadow with such strength, it made the trees groan as their branches swayed, and it set a few geese tumbling to the ground.

Davina shrieked and covered her face with her arms.

Rynn forced herself to stand tall despite being buffeted by the winds. "Enough." She made herself speak the word without trembling *or* shouting.

Instantly, the wind died down into a delightful breeze. The only evidence of its violence was in Rynn's and Davina's twisted skirts, and the white feathers a few geese had shed that now danced in the air.

"That was strange," Davina declared.

Rynn sat down, heedless of the grass and what it might do to her skirts. "I give up," she muttered. "I want to go home. I was so stupid for ever leaving."

Davina ignored her and instead walked up to a goose that was pecking at pebbles in a sandy patch next to the stream. "See here now, stop that!"

Rynn pushed the palms of her hands into her eyes and tried to pull herself together. *I can get through this. I know I can. Maybe I just need to work harder on Prince Geraint. If I could just get him out here to see Davina...but how will we deal with the truth?* She chewed on her lip. *Perhaps Lady Maela would help then. In spite of her distaste for Davina, I doubt she would try to continue the ruse if I managed to spill everything.*

Unfortunately, even though bringing Geraint and Davina together was by far her best idea, it had proven rather difficult to work on. Geraint was willing enough to ride, but he insisted on taking Conrad with them—who was never available until the evening hours, long after Davina and the geese returned to the palace.

Perhaps this is my punishment for bossing my siblings around and believing I could manage their lives better than they could. Hah. Now I can barely even survive living through mine. Rynn opened her eyes to find Davina wrestling with a goose.

"What are you doing?" Rynn asked.

"I'm saving this stupid bird's life," Davina grunted. "These silly geese keep trying to swallow rocks—ow!" She yelped when the goose flapped its wings and smacked her in the face. She let the bird go, which swallowed its pebble and honked in triumph.

Rynn pushed herself into a standing position again. "Just leave it be. Geese need to swallow pebbles and grit for their gizzards."

Davina stood and dusted off her palms. "What do the rocks do?"

"Grind their food so the goose can digest it," Rynn said. "Didn't they give you any instructions when they put you in charge of the gaggle?"

Davina shook her head and scrunched her nose. "No. They said all I had to do was assist the experienced goose boy. But Little Conrad replaced him the day after I arrived. I don't think he has much experience either."

Rynn turned around to peer at the goose lad, who had waded into the stream to cool off—though based on the direction his hat pointed, Rynn suspected he was watching them. "Putting two greenhorns together seems fair foolish..." *Foolish, and unlikely. No one would risk losing all the king's geese to beginner mistakes.*

"I thought so, too, but the man in charge of all the poultry won't listen to me," Davina sighed.

"I see. So neither of you truly know what you're doing?" Rynn asked.

Davina shook her head. "No."

Rynn briefly squeezed her eyes shut. *I should leave them alone. I have enough to worry about without adding goose-tending to my list...but to do something I'm familiar with would be so nice for a change!*

Geese had always been Rynn's least-favorite bird that her parents owned. They were big, pushy, and could be downright *mean*. But Rynn had managed her parents' birds for years before she left her family. As ornery as they were, the familiar honks and hisses of the geese soothed Rynn. *I never would have thought hissing geese would be the lullaby that reminds me of home.*

The goose Rynn had saved from Davina's misguided ministrations pecked at her skirt. Rynn exhaled, and a delightful little breeze played with her hair and rustled the leaves of the trees. "All right. I have nothing better to do." She turned on her heels and shouted. "Little Conrad, come! We're going to move the geese!"

"Move them where?" Davina asked.

Rynn pushed her already short sleeves up past her elbows. "Towards the trees. This direct sunlight is too strong for them in the summer heat. They should have the option of shade."

Little Conrad trotted up to them, pulling his cap low over his head. "We could take them to the Royal Orchard."

"It would be the ideal place for them," Rynn agreed. "But if the orchard has any young trees, the geese will strip the bark right off the trunks."

"How do you know that?" Davina asked, fascinated.

"Experience," Rynn said grimly. "Little Conrad and I will walk behind the geese and push them towards the trees. Vina, I want you to walk off to the side so you can keep them from circling around behind us."

Davina nodded and, to Rynn's surprise, skipped off without protesting.

Rynn and Little Conrad strode towards the geese, making them honk and waddle across the meadow.

Falada looked up from his grazing long enough to swat his tail as Rynn and Little Conrad drove the birds past him, then returned to grazing.

"How does a princess know so much about geese?" Little Conrad grunted, jumping back when a goose paused to peck at his shins.

Rynn opened her mouth to reply, but nothing would come out. *Stupid vow!* The breeze seemed to sense her frustration, for it tugged her hair into her face. Finally, Rynn replied. "I don't know."

CHAPTER 5
A VICIOUS THREAT

Rain fell in sheets as Rynn—a cloak pulled tight around her—hurried across the puddle-riddled courtyard. When she made it into the stables, she peeled the cloak off and hung it on a hook before she hurried down the aisleway.

"Falada," she called. "I'm sorry, but I don't think we'll get to ride today."

The fairy horse scratched his forehead on his stall door. "You think?" he asked sourly. "If that's so, what do you want?"

"I just wanted to let you know so you weren't waiting for me," Rynn said.

"I, wait for *you*?" Falada scoffed, arching his neck.

"Yes, I knew it was unlikely," Rynn muttered.

To her amusement, the gray pony housed in the stall on Falada's left strained her neck so she could poke her muzzle over the stall divider and sigh at him.

Falada recoiled at the pony's lovestruck expression and sneered.

Rynn cleared her throat, though a bit of a chuckle still leaked from her, creating a swirling breeze that tossed bits of hay into the air. She paused, but the fairy horse did not seem to mind it and instead continued to eye the pony.

"At least you won't be alone in here," Rynn ventured.

Falada ripped his attention from the pony and snorted. "The mushrooms are *not* fit company."

"Does that mean the other mushroom likes you, too?" Rynn asked, peering into the stall of the fat pony who was housed on Falada's other side.

"No!" Falada pawed his door and eyed Rynn.

Rynn froze for a moment, but Falada did not strike out at her or bite the flirtatious pony who was still trying to stick her head into his stall.

Maybe he's lonely, too. Even though he seems as ornery as ever, by now he should have bitten me.

Rynn cleared her throat and clasped her hands behind her back. "At least they're better than geese."

Falada tossed his head. "Don't you have somewhere else to be?"

"Not really."

Falada turned so his large, white rear faced Rynn. "Good day, Princess."

"Have the stable hands send for me if you want some company." Feeling brave, she ventured a slightly louder chuckle—one that mussed the forelock of Falada's pony admirer with the breeze it created.

Falada responded by swatting his tail.

Rynn shook her head and started back up the aisle. "Enjoy your afternoon!" She reclaimed her wet cloak from the hook, shivering as she wrapped it around herself again.

When she staggered across the courtyard that stretched between the stables and the palace, she sneezed, creating a gust of wind that almost knocked her flat.

Regardless of whether they fade or not, I have got to get Mortimer to take these powers back. If I get a cold, I'll flatten the palace! Though I don't have much hope of him retracting his gift—he never removed Eva's magic, and she has it worse than I do.

Rynn stumbled into the palace, squeezing her eyes shut as she tried to hold in another sneeze. She started to peel her cloak off when it subsided, then yelped when someone grabbed her by the shoulder and twisted her around.

Captain Hulderic smiled pleasantly. "Hello, Princess."

Rynn swallowed. "Captain."

"It's come to my attention that you go to the stables to ride nearly every day." The captain started down the dark, empty hallway, keeping Rynn at his side with his iron grip on her shoulder.

"Falada needs exercise, or he'll tear the stables apart," Rynn said.

"A believable excuse," Hulderic nodded, the soft smile plying his lips. "However, it does not explain why you visit the *goose meadow*."

Rynn sucked in a breath of air and felt an icy cold breeze sneak down her back. *He knows.* She scoffed at herself. *Of course he knows. Why else would he corner me in an apparently abandoned hallway.* "What do you care where Falada and I go?" Rynn tried to discreetly glance up and down the hallway.

Hulderic's grip on her shoulder tightened, going from uncomfortable to painful. She squirmed, but he did not release her. "You visit the meadow because that is where *Davina* is. You hope to talk her around, no doubt. But it's too late for that. You've run out of time."

Craning her neck, Rynn thought she saw an old man duck in the same entrance she had used behind them, but he immediately entered a side room. *This is too empty to be a coincidence. Hulderic must have planned for this.* "It's not too late," she said stubbornly. "King Othmar and Queen Morgaine will understand!"

Hulderic sighed. "So blind," he murmured.

Rynn tried to step away from him—she even considered kicking him—but Hulderic transferred his bruising grip from her shoulder to the back of her neck. Rynn squeaked and lunged forward, trying to dislodge him, but Hulderic dug his fingers into the side of her neck and hung on.

Whipping her back by the grip he had on her neck, Hulderic pulled her into his side. "Listen, *maid*," he sneered into her ear, his breath stirring a few strands of her hair. "Desist your meddling. If you step even one toe out of line, I will reveal you before the entire court."

Rynn narrowed her eyes. "If you do that, Davina will be arrested with me."

Hulderic smiled, the darkness in his eyes threatening to swallow up the world. "And you believe I care at all what happens to her? How *quaint* you are. No, as far as I am concerned, the princess can hang with you."

Horror spread through Rynn. *I've been so occupied trying to fix everything, I assumed Hulderic had some sort of romantic design on the princess...but I was wrong. He must have a far more insidious motivation...But if that's so, what do I do?*

Hulderic slid his fingers around the side of her neck so they dug into her windpipe. "Do you finally understand the situation, *princess?*"

It was hard to breathe around his fingers. Rynn pulled her leg back to kick him, and the captain flicked a dagger into the fingers of his free hand, sheltering it between their bodies so any passerby would not see it.

Rynn's blood turned into ice. *Do I scream? It will surely summon a huge wind, which will protect me, but it will also oust my magic. But I can't just do as he says!*

"It is to be hoped that you have a reasonable excuse for touching the princess," stated a calm, inflectionless voice.

Hulderic released Rynn's neck and tucked his dagger away before Rynn was able to turn and set her thankful eyes upon Conrad.

The enigmatic man held an unsheathed short sword and wore

an unreadable expression. He glanced at Rynn—his eyes lingering on her neck—before he turned all of his attention to Hulderic.

Hulderic bowed choppily. "Sir Conrad, I beg your pardon. Princess Davina and I were merely exchanging fond memories of our Astoria."

"And memories cause bruising?" Conrad inquired.

The monster of a captain tilted his head, then turned to Rynn and widened his eyes with false dismay. "Princess—how negligent of me, I had not noticed! What happened to your throat?"

Rynn rubbed her throat as her mind raced. *If I declare he did it, Conrad might believe me...but Hulderic will doubtlessly claim I am a fraud. If the princess agreed to testify as well, we might stand a chance. But as it is now, this might put me in a more dangerous position. Still...I cannot give in!*

She cleared her throat and forced a smile. "I'm afraid in the stables I ran afoul of a rather mad and *deranged* tom cat."

Hulderic's eyes glittered. He understood the promise.

"I see." Conrad did not look away from Rynn's neck, making her fidget with the intensity of his gaze. "Captain, you are dismissed."

Captain Hulderic bowed again and turned his back to Conrad. The corner of his lips edged down in a barely perceivable quirk as he glanced at Rynn and wrapped his hand around the hilt of his sword. He strode off in a slight swagger, the set of his shoulders and the confidence of his stride making Rynn want to gnash her teeth.

It wasn't until Hulderic disappeared into a side hallway that Conrad finally sheathed his sword, and Rynn found she could breathe normally.

"You visited the stables?" Conrad asked, nodding his head at her wet cloak.

Rynn tried to peel it off her. "Yes. I wanted to make certain Falada was comfortable...both for his good as well as for the well-being of the stable."

Conrad nodded slowly. "A wise decision." He squatted down and pulled the wet cloak from the skirts of Rynn's dress, helping her shed the sopping garment.

"Thank you." Rynn flicked raindrops from her hair and smiled. She had to stiffen her spine to keep from shivering.

Conrad raised an eyebrow. "Are you cold?"

"I am fine," Rynn lied.

He ignored her and instead narrowed his eyes while he studied her. "No, you are cold. Stay here a moment." He took Rynn's soaked cape from her and retreated down the hallway.

She shifted uneasily in the silence, peering suspiciously in the direction Hulderic had meandered. *I hope he does not return.*

"Here."

Rynn jumped a little in surprise, then shuffled around to face Conrad, who held a hunter-green cloak.

"Oh, thank you!" Rynn eagerly reached for it, but Conrad backed out of reach and motioned for her to turn around.

Rynn slowly did so, and Conrad draped the cloak over her shoulders, fussing with the cloth so it properly enfolded her. She instantly felt warmer—though she still had to stifle the desire to shudder from Hulderic's threat.

"You will tell me if you have any worries or troubles?" Conrad asked.

Surprised, Rynn turned around and discovered he had not backed away after helping her with the cloak. Instead, he stood rather *close*. She gulped. *He is taller than I realized,* she thought as he loomed next to her. "I'm afraid it's nothing I can explain at the moment."

He nodded slowly, though there was a strange light in his dark eyes. "I see."

Does he maybe suspect...?

He leaned closer, and Rynn found she couldn't look away. In fact, as he scrutinized her, his eyes thoughtfully tracing her face, she had the very untimely realization that Conrad, for all his reserve, was rather handsome.

The closer he leaned, the warmer Rynn felt, and the brighter that strange light in his eyes became.

Enough silliness! Rynn scolded herself. *I will soon sound like Davina.*

The edges of Conrad's lips quirked up, and he pulled away, only to offer Rynn his arm.

Rynn hesitated. Though Princess Lunette and Queen Morgaine embraced her freely, thus far, Geraint was the only male who had offered his arm. She had assumed it was something to do with being his fiancée. *Perhaps it is simply that they are a reserved family?*

Rynn meekly tucked her arm in the crook of Conrad's elbow, her shoulders stooping a little in her relief. Conrad was warm and reassuring, pushing the memory of Hulderic's icy fingers digging into her throat from her mind.

She waited for Conrad to lead the way down the hallway, but he paused for a moment, then pulled his arm from her grip and instead took her hand and intertwined it with his.

Rynn glanced up at him in surprise, but Conrad was faced resolutely forward, his expression as blank as ever as he started down the hallway, gently tugging her along.

He's much kinder than one would think. Rynn walked hand-in-hand with him. A smile nearly dawned on her face until she recalled the situation in which she met him. *Hopefully he and the rest of the royal family are also more understanding than one would think. Or Hulderic just might win no matter what I do. And that*, she thought grimly, *seems to be his only aim.*

RYNN SAT ON A LOG, her chin resting on her propped-up fist,

watching Davina serenade the geese with a long-winded Caladonian ballad about mermaids luring sailors to their death.

Davina's voice was admittedly sweet and pleasant to listen to. The ballad wasn't one Rynn much cared for, but she found herself listening wistfully to the princess. "Maybe she really could be a minstrel."

Little Conrad, who was perched on the same log and eating wild strawberries he carried in a kerchief, snorted. "She'd be robbed blind on a weekly basis. If not daily."

Rynn smiled and stifled the desire to chuckle. "In all likelihood, yes."

"Inn owners would cheat her out of her earnings," the boy added.

One of the geese honked at Davina as she waltzed past him, her sweet voice rising and falling with the crystalline notes of the song. The princess turned in a neat circle, her hands gliding through the air.

"We can always hope her desire to be a minstrel does not outlast the persistence needed to earn the coins for her lyre," Rynn said. (Over her many visits to the goose meadow, she had identified the goose boy as an ally, for though he was young, he possessed all the sense Davina lacked and rather reminded her of an old man.)

"Certainly," Little Conrad said. "And I might secretly be a lord who has grand plans to sweep you off your feet."

A peal of laughter finally escaped Rynn with such force she almost slipped off the back of the log.

The wind whipped up by her laughter flung Davina's hair into her face and even yanked Little Conrad's cap off his head. The goose boy hopped off the log and chased after his cap as the wind carried it across the meadow, mussing his ashy brown hair. Several of the geese chased after him, honking and cackling before they were distracted by a patch of sweet grass and stopped their chase.

Davina cut off her song and instead launched into a string of curse words she most assuredly *hadn't* know before her career as a goose girl. Her face still obscured by her curtain of golden hair, she tripped on a goose that nibbled on her apron as she righted herself.

Little Conrad finally caught his cap at the far side of the meadow and shoved it back on his head, making Rynn—who was holding her sides to keep in additional laughter at the chaos her first chortle had caused—realize it was the first moment she saw his head uncovered. *He does love that hat.*

"The wind here is so *unpredictable*," Davina complained as she smoothed her hair back into place. She plopped down next to Rynn on the log and sighed.

A smile still played at the edges of Rynn's mouth. She glanced at Conrad, who was fishing a goose out from a patch of prickery black raspberry canes after the bird had been tossed there by the wind.

"Vina..." Rynn began.

"Please, do not start." Davina's voice was not haughty, but instead tight—as if unshed tears clogged her throat. "I am tired of being told I am not bright enough to handle myself."

Rynn glanced at the princess in surprise. "That's not what I wanted to talk to you about."

Davina twisted to face her. "Oh?"

Rynn shook her head. "No. I wanted to talk about Captain Hulderic. I think there's something...off about him."

"What do you mean?"

"He threatened me," Rynn said.

Davina—who was barefoot—dug her toes into the grass and dirt. "Did you tell him you were going to reveal the truth? I imagine he did so out of loyalty to my family."

"No, it's more than that. He made it clear he doesn't care what happens to either of us. I don't think he's loyal at all. I think you and I are just pieces in his plan."

"Impossible," Davina scoffed. "Captain Hulderic has been

nothing but helpful and thoughtful since I approached him about my plan. He told me what other men could be bribed into silence and suggested swapping places with you."

"Yes, but would someone loyal to your family let you wander off into a new life without any sort of protection? You were robbed, Davina, but it could have been much worse. Any soldier would *know* that."

Davina pressed her lips together.

"Furthermore, a soldier who is honorable and willing to lay down his life for his country would *not* be willing to risk that same country by attempting to pass off a maid for a princess." Rynn hesitated, afraid to say too much and draw Davina's stubbornness to the front.

To all appearances, her words had not reached the princess at all. She did not look at Rynn but stared out at the meadow, her lips pursed. But Rynn saw the faint wrinkle in her brow, which stirred hope in her.

She's thinking about it...she's starting to see it. It would do, for now. Rynn would bring the matter before Lady Maela as well—if she could ever corner her again.

"Princess Davina," Little Conrad shouted. "One of the geese is limping."

Rynn stood up and brushed off her skirts. "Coming!" She glanced down at Davina again, then meandered towards Little Conrad, the grass tickling her bared ankles. Rynn was almost to the goose boy and his charge when she glanced past him, at the shadows of the forest.

She stilled when she saw Hulderic, mounted on a dark horse, standing in the gloom of the trees.

Hulderic held her gaze as he flipped a dagger in the air and shook his head.

How long has he been watching?

Rynn's heart squeezed in her chest as he turned his horse and disappeared into the thickness of the woods.

Little Conrad squinted up at her, then turned to see what she was staring at.

Rynn doubted he saw Hulderic—he certainly didn't say anything—but he scratched his head through his cap and stared at the woods longer than Rynn did.

Shivering slightly, Rynn placed a hand over her heart and tried to breathe normally to keep the wind steady. *Maybe I should talk to Prince Geraint and Conrad...tonight.*

CHAPTER 6
THE TRUTH

Rynn tried in vain to speak to Prince Geraint and Conrad privately, but fate, it seemed, was persistent in thwarting her.

Neither the prince nor Conrad were at dinner that evening.

She did not see Prince Gertaint until the following morning to discuss wedding plans with Queen Morgaine. The prince seemed distracted and barely listened to two words Morgaine or Rynn said. The queen sent him away before Rynn could ask for a private audience with him.

Conrad was even less available. Rynn saw him once with his father and King Othmar, but before Rynn could approach him, the trio entered the king's private study.

To make matters worse, Lady Maela was unavailable as well. No matter when Rynn visited, it seemed like the lady was always out in Cadburey or off on a day trip to a smaller town or village. (Lady Maela's absence was most disappointing, given that she did seem truly concerned for the country. If she learned what a wretch Hulderic was, perhaps she would change her mind!)

Rynn hunched her shoulders up to her chin as she slowly

trekked across the courtyard, making for the stables. *I feel like a mouse scurrying from a cat.*

Hulderic's look had been unmistakable. Since she had not listened to his warning and continued to visit Davina, he was going to do something in retribution.

If I could just catch Conrad alone for a moment! Rynn frowned and kicked a rock before she slipped into the stables, shuffling toward Falada's stall.

The fairy horse chewed a mouthful of hay and watched her draw closer. "What's wrong?"

Rynn leaned against his stall door and shook her head. She closed her eyes, cursing her inability to even sigh! *Some gift. Mortimer must truly be the worst fairy godfather in history. If I survive this and ever see my parents again, I shall apologize profusely for thinking they were dunces for scorning his gifts.*

All thoughts fled her mind, however, when a velvet muzzle pressed against her temple. Rynn was afraid to move a muscle, lest Falada change his expression of sympathy into a bite.

"Tell Conrad as much as you can," the fairy horse said into her hair.

Rynn blinked. "The goose boy?"

"No. The adult."

Rynn scrunched her brow and turned to him, hesitating only a moment before placing her hand on Falada's left cheek. "How do you know Conrad?"

"He comes every night to see that I am well cared for."

"Has he been doing this since we arrived?"

Falada lipped her hair. "No. Only since we began visiting the goose meadows regularly. There is magic on him."

"*Conrad?*" Rynn asked, unable to believe *Conrad*—the most stable and expressionless member of the royal family—had received a fairy gift or wish. Particularly given he was from Farthendale!

Before Falada could respond, a holster, whistling merrily as he strode down the hallway, approached them. "Good day to you, Princess! Would you like one of the lads to saddle Falada for you?"

Rynn stepped away from the door and smiled. "Yes, please."

The holster motioned for one of the stable boys, who trotted down the aisle to retrieve Falada's saddle.

The holster reached into the stall next to Falada's and patted the gray pony—the one enamored with the fairy horse. "It's a grand thing to see your friendship," he said, nodding first at Rynn and then at Falada. "I've met lots of riders who trust their mounts, but you two?"

The holster opened the stall door for the stable boy, who worked quickly but did not quake with the fear many of the boys had initially approached Falada with.

When did it change? Rynn wondered. *It's been a long while since I've feared he would throw me...when did* that *change? But are we really as close as the holster seems to think?*

The stable boy had Falada bridled and saddled in no time and handed the reins off to Rynn.

"Enjoy your ride, princess." The holster and stable boy bowed, then returned to their duties.

Rynn loosely held one rein and led the way out of the stable and into the brilliant sunlight. "Are you sure you don't want to bring a pony friend along?" she asked.

"I *will* bite you."

Rynn grinned and bit her lip to keep from laughing. She tossed Falada's reins over his head, but just before she was about to scramble her way into the saddle, she saw Prince Geraint stroll out of the palace and into the courtyard. "Geraint," Rynn called.

The prince briefly shielded his eyes, then strolled in her direction. "Davina, good day to you! You are looking as lovely as ever."

"Thank you. I am glad to see you—I feel like we haven't spoken in a while." Rynn offered the prince her friendliest smile.

"Ahh, yes." The prince awkwardly scratched the back of his neck. "You know how it is...royal duties and everything."

He seems as friendly as usual, but over the course of our acquaintance, he has certainly become less interested in me in general. Rynn brushed off the observation. "I was wondering if it is possible to meet you—and Sir Conrad—later today."

Geraint tilted his head and focused his attention on Rynn, his brow wrinkling in concern. "Certainly. I hope everything is all right?"

Rynn nodded. "Yes, it is only—"

"There she is, Your Majesty!"

Rynn felt the cold fingers of fear spread through her body at the sound of Captain Hulderic's voice. Her knees trembling, Rynn swiveled to face her accuser.

Storming across the courtyard was Captain Hulderic, King Othmar, Lord Medrod, and a number of guards.

"There's the traitor," Hulderic declared, pointing directly to her.

Rynn took a step backwards, smacking into Falada's side. *Is he trying to get me arrested? But why? I expected him to attack me at night—not this!*

"Blast!" Geraint muttered. Rynn glanced at him in surprise, but the prince wore a look of confusion. "What is going on, Father?"

King Othmar's brows lowered, and he shook his head. "Captain Hulderic claims that Princess Davina is not who she says she is."

Rynn stared blankly in surprise. "W-what?" she stammered. *No! He can't mean to reveal my real identity to the king. Lady Maela will naysay him! What is he doing?* Fear threatened to close Rynn's throat just as effectively as Hulderic's fist had when he last spoke with her.

Geraint laughed—though it sounded a tad forced. "What a ridiculous accusation!"

"He claims she is really a maid who is merely *pretending* to be the princess. Apparently the Astorian queen values her daughter so much, she did not want to throw her away on a marriage to you." Based on the King's dry tone, he didn't wholly believe Hulderic, but Rynn didn't like the way he studied her either, as if she were a felon brought forward for his judgement.

"Indeed," Hulderic piously bowed his head. "It was Queen Cassia who instructed us to carry out this farce. She intends to impose new importation taxes and has already begun secretly mining the mountains in the north." Hulderic morosely wrinkled his forehead. "I could not continue with this charade anymore. Since I have arrived, Your Majesty, your country has been nothing but kind and welcoming. What the Queen plans is not right, and I cannot stand by and see her ruin you!"

Is he mad? Has he lost all sense? I can see revealing me, but how can he hope to convince them all of this ridiculous falsehood? "That's not true." Rynn wanted to scream, but showing off her unwanted magic would only make things worse. Instead, she forced herself to stand tall. "Queen Cassia would *never* do such a thing!"

"Do you see how she calls her Queen Cassia, not her mother?" Hulderic shook his head.

"Stop lying," Rynn snapped. A stiff breeze whisked through the courtyard, but no one seemed to take notice of it. "I don't know what he's trying to accomplish, Your Majesty, but Astoria has no ulterior plans or motives! Call for Lady Maela; she will explain everything!"

"A sound suggestion!" Geraint motioned at one of the guards, who trotted off into the castle.

"I'm afraid it only gets worse," Hulderic added. "Not only did Queen Cassia send an impersonator, but this *maid* has mag—"

"Surely you do not believe this drabble," Falada interrupted Hulderic with his low, gravelly voice. "What proof does this *guard* have?"

King Othmar's expression was no longer quite so impassive. Instead, he rubbed his chin as he studied Rynn. "Captain?"

"The portrait sent last year is of the real Davina—who is as beautiful as the morning sun," Hulderic said. "But you can see it in other ways—her ill-fitting dress, her lack of refinement. But, more importantly, I have the collaboration of my men."

Hulderic's men—who were interspersed with the Farthendale soldiers—raised their fists. "Aye!"

"Such solid research you have shown," Falada sneered. "And how convincing it is that *your men*—whom you handpicked—agree with you."

"Then you disagree with the charges Hulderic has presented?" King Othmar asked the fairy horse.

Falada raised his head to his full height and arched his neck, making him look even more splendid than usual. "Astoria has done none of the planning or scheming this dolt accuses of them."

Rynn placed a hand on Falada's muscled shoulder, thankful for the horse's intervention.

"But you do not deny the princess is not who she says she is?" King Othmar asked.

Falada turned his neck slightly so he could glance back at Rynn. "My rider is filled with honor and a desire to do whatever is right. The *captain* only has a desire to nurture conflict and terror."

"You are a *horse*," Hulderic sneered. "What do *you* know?"

Falada lunged at the captain with murder in his eyes.

"Falada!" Rynn grabbed his reins and tried to pull him back, grimacing as the wind howled in her ears. *This is bad. Even after Hulderic's treachery is remedied, I still may be revealed as having magic!*

"Lady Maela!" announced the guard Geraint had dispatched earlier.

King Othmar raised an eyebrow and hooked a thumb on his gold belt. "Finally, someone who can perhaps shed some light on this delicate situation."

Rynn sagged into Falada's side, light-hearted with relief.

Finally. Lady Maela will fix this. Hulderic will suffer, and perhaps the real reason for his actions can be wrestled from him!

Lady Maela's snowy hair gleamed as she joined the impromptu court session in the courtyard. She did not look at Rynn or Hulderic but instead curtsied to the King. "Your Majesty."

King Othmar acknowledged her with a flick of his hand. "Lady Maela, please put an end to this madness and tell me, are Captain Hulderic's accusations false?"

Rynn took a careful breath—breathing slowly to keep from stirring the wind.

"I'm afraid, Your Majesty," Lady Maela began, "it's all true."

WHAT? Shocked, Rynn gaped at Lady Maela, her ears ringing and her mind blank.

The ambassador sighed and folded her hands in front of her. "This girl is not Davina, and Astoria has been preparing for several years to end our dependency upon Farthendale goods. I fear my queen has played you, Your Majesty."

Rynn felt the trap snap shut on her. Suddenly, it all made sense. Lady Maela had been Davina's confidante from the beginning—she had even recommended the soldiers Davina could bribe. *All this time, Hulderic was not acting in his own interests...but Lady Maela's! But why?*

"I am sorry it took my conscience this long to bring the truth forward," Lady Maela continued. "It is my failing as a human—I should have warned you long before."

I can't believe this. They really do mean to bring ruin! Rynn briefly closed her eyes and pictured her family home and her siblings—not just Eva, but all of her precious sisters and her single brother. *What happens to me is irrelevant. This is much bigger than Davina and I now.*

"Lady Maela is lying," Rynn said, her voice stronger than she felt. "Queen Cassia has nothing to do with this. Astoria is not mining the mountains or planning to cut off trade with you."

"I believe her, Father." Geraint took a step closer to Rynn.

"You believe a girl who might be a lady's maid over an ambassador we have known for years?" King Othmar asked.

"Yes," Geraint said.

May all the fairies in the world bless Geraint...although maybe he would be better off if they didn't. Rynn smiled gratefully at Geraint, but the prince only nodded at her.

"Believe what you like, Your Majesty. Farthendale is your responsibility." Lady Maela turned to face Rynn, her eyes icy cold. "But I swear upon all I own this girl is *not* Princess Davina."

"Is this true?" King Othmar asked, shifting his steely gaze to Rynn. "You are not Davina?"

Rynn opened her mouth, but no words would come. *I'm still under that awful vow! Blast it, Davina! I hope all of your gorgeous hair falls out of your head!* She shook her head and wove her fingers through Falada's thick mane.

"Who are you?" King Othmar pressed.

"Falada, can you tell the truth?" Rynn murmured to the fairy horse.

The horse pawed at the ground. "I could, but the crossbows aimed on us might bring the end before I can explain everything."

Alarmed by his observation, Rynn jerked her gaze to the soldiers. Sure enough, she saw several guards—two of Hulderic's and a number of Farthendellans—holding loaded crossbows pointed at them.

Hulderic folded his arms across his chest. "Do you see, Your Majesty, how cagey she is?"

"You cannot wholly blame the girl—she was only doing as she was ordered," Lady Maela said. "Though it is not to her credit that she insists on continuing with the sham."

King Othmar motioned for silence. "I will ask you once more," he said to Rynn. "Who. Are. You?"

"I'm, I'm..." Rynn stammered.

One of Hulderic's soldiers raised his crossbow, clearly aiming for her.

Falada snorted and charged in front of Rynn, shielding her.

"Take the animal down!" Hulderic shouted to his men.

"No!" Rynn screamed. The wind roared to life, buffeting through the courtyard with such power, it nearly ripped the decorative flags from their poles.

"Do you see, Your Majesty!" Captain Hulderic shouted. "This imposter even has magic!"

"Arrest her," Lady Maela clung to a guard to keep from stumbling as the wind howled and swirled.

"Attempt it, and you will pay!" Falada snarled. He looked wilder than usual as the wind whipped his tail and mane. "Rynn, mount up. We have to get out of here."

Rynn shook her head as the wind finally started to subside. "I can't! If I run, they'll win!"

"Do you see, Your Majesty?" Hulderic shouted. "She is a menace! Regardless of how guilty you should hold her for this farce, she must be locked up due to her magical grasp of wind!"

Falada circled around Rynn, screaming a challenge at the captain.

Rynn rolled her shoulders back. "I'm not Davina!" She was shocked when the words tumbled from her mouth—it was probably because Hulderic and Lady Maela had revealed as much. "My name is Corynn. But Lady Maela and Captain Hulderic are lying! The real Davina is—" Rynn choked when her throat closed and the words would no longer come.

King Othmar and Prince Geraint stared at each other. Geraint looked from Rynn to his father. King Othmar shrugged and shook his head.

Lady Maela smoothed her hair. "Your Majesty, I recommend you place the girl in jail and focus on what matters—the treachery of Queen Cassia."

"Please, Your Majesty. They're lying! You must believe me," Rynn begged. Her breath hitched, making the breeze stir unnaturally again.

"Men, fire on my command!" Hulderic shouted.

Falada reared, knocking Geraint over as he again moved to stand in front of Rynn.

"Falada—no!" Rynn shouted.

Hulderic's two soldiers who had crossbows raised them, aiming at Falada and Rynn.

Ice spread through Rynn. *This is it. They're going to kill me in this chaos!* She grabbed Falada's reins and tried to drag him away, but she saw the soldiers's fingers inch towards the bow release.

"STOP!" a youthful voice shouted.

Rynn whirled around and was slightly shocked to see Little Conrad and Davina hurrying across the courtyard. "Vina?"

Little Conrad was wearing clothes that were so big on him, they looked like they were meant for a grown man. Davina still wore her goose girl uniform, though her hair was prettily braided, and she peered around the palace courtyard with wide eyes.

The princess paused in front of Geraint long enough to smile prettily at him as he stood up. When the prince shyly returned the smile, Little Conrad grabbed Davina by the wrist and dragged her to Rynn.

"Vina, what are you doing here?" Rynn asked. She was glad to see her, but it was dangerous. *She can't say who she is either, and now Hulderic and Lady Maela will be able to kill her as well!*

Little Conrad released his grasp on Davina's wrist and reached out and squeezed Rynn's hand in reassurance. "Everything will be fine," he said.

"Are you *mad*?" Rynn hissed. "I'm being accused of impersonating a princess; there's a crossbow aimed at Falada and me; and it turns out the Astorian ambassador is a *traitor*!"

Little Conrad merely shook his head and squeezed her hand again.

"Ahh, Conrad. I was wondering what kept you." King Othmar's voice was once again pleasant as he smiled at the goose boy. "What have you found, nephew?"

Rynn blinked. "What?"

Little Conrad hunched over, falling into a forward roll. When he popped out of the maneuver, he was much older and much taller, and his clothes fit perfectly, though his ashy brown hair was the same shade.

"Conrad?" Rynn yelped, shocked by the transformation. "But you just...how?"

Prince Geraint grinned as he offered his cousin a handshake. "You certainly took your time." He turned to Rynn and explained. "Conrad once saved two children from a cannibal witch. A fairy godmother gave him a blessing in return: the ability to change his appearance to whatever age he wishes."

"That seems like a useful gift." Davina eyed Conrad as he tugged his clothes straight. "You could be young forever."

"I'm afraid it's appearances only. He still ages like the rest of us." Geraint turned to his cousin. "Don't keep us in suspense, old boy. Tell us everything!"

"Captain Hulderic and Lady Maela's story is a mixture of truths and lies," Conrad said. "Astoria has no plans to break off trading with us or raise any additional taxes."

"You are certain of this?" King Othmar asked.

Conrad nodded. "I saw Captain Hulderic assaulting the princess's stand-in while infiltrating the palace. I also overheard Lady Maela colluding with him as well."

It took Rynn a moment to recall that when Conrad had saved her during her previous encounter with the disloyal captain, she had seen an elderly man in the hallway before his sudden arrival.

"He is lying, Your Majesty." Lady Maela shook her head and sighed heavily. "The traitor perhaps has swayed him to her side."

King Othmar frowned. "You accuse my nephew of being a traitor as well?"

Lady Maela's smile was patient and grandmotherly as she folded her hands together. "I would not say that, but he is simply not telling the truth. What advantage would I have in telling you Queen Cassia's plans?"

"You mean besides the fact that you own the bulk of the mining rights to the mountains?" Conrad asked blankly. "And that if you succeeded in turning Farthendale against Astoria, you would be made very rich if you became the biggest provider of precious metals to your own countrymen?"

Lady Maela stilled. Though she continued to smile, it looked brittle. "That's preposterous. I have no lands—it was why I was chosen to be an ambassador."

"And your position is how you were able to buy up all the rights over the last decade." Sir Medrod shook his head and leaned back on his heels. "You've been playing a *very* long-term game, Maela."

"Guards, arrest Lady Maela, Captain Hulderic, and his men for conspiring against the Astorian Royal Family," King Othmar declared.

The Farthendale soldiers who stood behind Hulderic's men with loaded crossbows—in what had *appeared* to be a gesture of unity—fanned around the captain and his men, their expressions grim and the bolts loaded in their crossbows glinting in the afternoon light.

Hulderic snarled, but he dropped his sword and knelt, his men mimicking him. "This was all her plan," he said, nodding at Maela. "I was only following orders!"

"Likely, I'm sure," Prince Geraint said.

The four guards that had escorted Lady Maela turned to her, their weapons drawn.

Lady Maela's brow wrinkled, and she pinched her face so her smooth skin twisted into an ugly sneer of hatred. "Keep your hands off me! You can't arrest me! You are not my sovereign, nor do you have any proof of your false accusations!"

King Othmar gestured to Sir Medrod, who plucked a scroll from his belt.

Sir Medrod cleared his voice. "Under the orders of Her Majesty Queen Cassia of Astoria, Lady Maela is arrested for charges of conspiring against the country of Astoria."

Lady Maela's face turned a chilling white that almost matched her hair. "How?" She howled.

"Lady Maela, you didn't honestly think the only way I communicated with Queen Cassia was through *you*, did you?" King Othmar asked.

Lady Maela howled in anger as the soldiers dragged her away.

"She blackmailed me," Captain Hulderic shouted as his arms were tied behind his back. "And don't you forget about the viper pretending to be Princess Davina! She's just as much a traitor as the rest of us, and she has *magic*!"

Rynn swallowed and grabbed Davina's hand in a death grip.

"Ow, you're hurting me," the princess complained.

Rynn ignored her and instead flicked her eyes back and forth between Hulderic and King Othmar.

"Enough of his howling," King Othmar said. "Take him away."

"But she's a traitor!" Hulderic snarled. He tried to lunge at Rynn, but a soldier grabbed him by the arms and yanked him backwards. "She knew of the whole plan! Ask her—she can't say no! She deserves to be sealed into a barrel of nails—"

Conrad grabbed Hulderic by the throat. "Utter one more threat to her—no—a *single* word about her, and I will see to it that our jailers know it is not necessary to send you back to Astoria *alive*." He pushed the soldier backwards, making him fall and curse when he hit the unforgiving stone ground.

Hulderic glared darkly in Rynn's direction.

Conrad stepped between them, to Rynn's relief. She couldn't see his expression as his back was to her, but he took a sword from a soldier and idly twirled it as Hulderic turned green and seemed to shrink in on himself.

"Take him away," Conrad ordered.

Rynn took in a shuddering breath—which made a ripple of

wind—and her heart soared. *I'm safe. I don't know how we'll muddle through explaining everything, but they know I didn't work with Lady Maela and her ilk.*

"Your enthusiasm for this series of arrests is noted, Conrad," King Othmar said.

"It is a great win," Prince Geraint said. He smiled at Davina, and it seemed he could not take his eyes off her, even though he spoke to his father. "It's taken us several years to pin down exactly *how* all the communication exchanges with Astoria seemed to go sideways and muddy."

"To think, it was the ambassador—the esteemed noble who is supposed to foster the relationship." Lord Medrod frowned as he watched the guards drag Hulderic and his men away. "Astorians must think us uncultured swine if he believes magic would be a black mark against you."

"It's not?" Davina asked—the only one with the strength to speak, as Rynn was still light-headed with relief.

"Of course not," King Othmar snorted. "Conrad has magic, and he's the royal spymaster. We just don't have much of it—he's one of the only beings in the country with a fairy blessing."

"Speaking of which, we may have arrested the ringleader, but this is far from over." Lord Medrod scuffed his boot and squinted up at the sun.

Conrad frowned and finally returned his attention to the conversation when the last traitorous Astorian guard was frog-marched into the palace. "What do you mean?"

"You are referring to the princess, I imagine?" King Othmar asked.

"Yes," Sir Medrod said. "Where's the real one?"

Conrad shrugged and looked to Davina.

Rynn groaned. "We're *still* stuck?"

Davina turned to Rynn with slightly furrowed brows. "You haven't told them yet?"

"I *can't*," Rynn growled. "Because of that ridiculous vow you made me take."

"You mean you haven't figured out the loophole?" Davina asked.

"What loophole?"

Davina laughed and giddily clapped her hands. "Worry not, Your Majesty," she called to King Othmar. "I will soon explain the situation."

Falada chewed on his bit. "And *how* do you expect to do that? No one has yet revealed all the truth. You won't be able to talk about it."

"To a living soul, yes," Davina said, "but there's nothing stopping me from telling that barrel." She pointed to an empty barrel tipped onto its side. "For it is not a living soul."

Pain assaulted Rynn's head in a sharp wave. "You must be joking."

Davina knelt gracefully in front of the barrel. "I am telling my story to this fine barrel," she said loud enough for all to hear. "I'm sure it will be glad to know that I am, in fact, Princess Davina of Astoria, and the lovely lady—who is not my equal in beauty though she is still rather fine looking—is my lady's maid, Corynn."

Davina explained her plot to live as an heiress—though she refrained from mentioning the fear that Geraint might be a hunchback spurred her into it—and how she had come to be employed as a goose girl, as well as Rynn's frequent trips to visit her.

Her tale to the barrel—which let everyone hear—loosened Rynn's tongue. "Davina?" Rynn said slowly, savoring the moment.

Davina turned away from the barrel and smiled merrily. "Yes?"

Rynn fell to her knees in her light-headed relief, landing next to her. "It worked," she gasped. "It really worked!" She stiffened when a breeze flicked her hair, having been summoned by the shortness of her breath.

"Of course it worked, silly," Davina giggled. "I chose my phrasing carefully when I gave that vow."

"What do you mean?" Rynn asked.

Davina patted Rynn's back in sympathy. "I thought we should leave an opening in case things went poorly, and I needed to speak to the king and take responsibility. Really, Corynn," she continued. "I'm hurt you thought I would foist all the weight upon you! Though I would be lying if I said I'm not proud that for once I managed to outsmart you."

Rynn had to press her lips together to keep her jaw from trembling as she studied the princess. "You mean you wouldn't have let me be punished in your stead?"

"Of course not." Davina slid an arm around Rynn's shoulders and briefly rested her head against Rynn's. "You're my only friend."

Rynn laughed, making the branches of the few decorative shrubs that dotted the courtyard sway with a breeze. "Thank you."

"You're welcome."

Prince Geraint cleared his throat and clasped his hands behind his back. "I find it disagreeable that I must interrupt your private conversation, but...Princess Davina?"

Davina straightened and put on her best smile. "Yes. You are Prince Geraint?"

He nodded.

"I apologize for my deception," Davina said. "I cannot tell you how much I regret it, how much I wish I *hadn't* listened to Lady Maela."

"Does this mean you are interested in marriage?" Prince Geraint asked.

"If you will have me." Davina's blue eyes glowed as she stared up into the prince's face with rapt attention.

Prince Geraint took her hand and kissed it. "It would be my honor." He offered her his arm. She took it, and neither of them could look away as they glided towards the palace, completely taken with each other.

Rynn watched the couple go, a tiny but fond smile briefly budding on her lips. *I'm glad. Everything is going to work out in spite of the upheaval. But now...what will happen to me?*

The original plan was that Rynn would return to Astoria after Davina was wed to Prince Geraint and settled in Farthendale. Assumedly, that was once again the plan, but what was she supposed to do until then?

Rynn turned in a circle, watching the Farthendale soldiers scurry around at the beck of their king, who was speaking to the guard who had escorted Lady Maela to the dungeon and had since returned. Lord Medrod and Conrad were cloistered off to the side—probably exchanging observations.

"That was an unexpected series of events," Falada rumbled in his deep, earthy voice.

"Indeed." Rynn rubbed her eyes, mentally exhausted though she summoned a tired smile for the fairy horse. "I expect when Lady Maela and Captain Hulderic are returned to Astoria and Queen Cassia learns of Davina's activities, she will write her a scathing letter."

Falada snorted. "She deserves it."

Rynn chuckled. "Perhaps, but I'm glad she came forward when she did."

Falada chewed his bit and said nothing, but he took a step closer to Rynn and sniffed her pockets—probably looking for the apples she occasionally smuggled out for him and the Mushrooms. Rynn draped an arm over his neck, taking strength from the sour horse as the rest of the world seemed to surge ahead without her.

I want to go home.

As THE DAY PROGRESSED, it soon became apparent no one had much use for Rynn. Davina was rightfully given the room meant for her and spent the afternoon with Prince Geraint and Queen Morgaine, chatting with her fiancé and ingratiating herself with the queen.

King Othmar, Lord Medrod, and Conrad were all busy meting out justice and flushing out any leftover Astorian contacts who had been aware of Lady Maela's ploy.

With no room to return to, no one to talk to, and no real purpose to fulfill, Rynn was left to aimlessly wander the palace. Eventually, she sought out solace in the least place imaginable—the stables.

Rynn chewed on a straw stem, sinking further into the straw pile she had arranged for herself.

The munch of horses chewing on hay was a comforting sound as she scratched her nose, finally feeling safe for the first time that day. She cast a glance at her unlikely guard dog, Falada, who was angled slightly towards her, even though he had to twist his neck uncomfortably to snatch a new mouthful of hay from his hay rack whenever he finished.

He ignored her look, and instead shook his head when one of the amorous mushrooms tried to poke her velveteen muzzle into his stall.

Chuckling, Rynn closed her eyes and held in the sigh she wanted to heave. *I should be happy. Besides my stupid wind magic, I got everything I wished for. I'm not being exiled or punished, and I'll soon return home and see my family...* "So why do I feel sad?" she murmured.

"Perhaps it is because you feel like a used sack of potatoes," Falada suggested. "In which case, I sympathize."

Rynn glanced curiously up at the fairy horse, who still wouldn't look at her and instead yanked another mouthful of hay free. "You don't like belonging to the royal family?" she asked.

"I don't like being a *pawn* trotted out for the occasions in which they wish to remind everyone how the fairies favor them," Falada sneered.

"Ahh," Rynn said in understanding. She stared up at the bright wooden ceiling of the barn. "Do you mind if I stay here tonight, Falada?"

"Surely they will provide you a room if you ask," Falada said

"Yes," Rynn agreed. "If I approach a servant, I'm sure they'll find something for me." They would also show her where the servants ate and help her return to her post as lady's maid, a thought that increased Rynn's desire to sigh and magically be home so she could cry into her mother's shoulder, laugh with Sophia, talk with Ellie, and maybe pat Martin's cheeks before he shrugged her off. *It's not that I think I'm above my old role...it is only...I truly liked Prince Geraint, King Othmar, Queen Morgaine, and Lord Medrod. It is sad that, with a return to my old job, I will never be of a status at which I will be able to speak to them again.*

There was one name in that list Rynn was dearly missing, but it would take wild horses to drag Conrad's name from her. Even acknowledging that thought made her want to snarl.

She rolled onto her side and cushioned her head on her arm. When she was finally comfortable, she closed her eyes.

"What do *you* want?" Falada sneered.

Rynn opened one eye and watched the horse slightly rearrange himself so his legs were braced, and he faced the stall door.

"Her," a male said.

Rynn's other eye popped open when she recognized his voice. She craned her neck, trying to peer past Falada's pinned ears and massive head to glimpse Conrad standing in the aisleway. "Conrad?" She sat up, brushing straw from her clothes.

Falada glanced back at her, then stiffly stepped aside so she could approach the door.

Conrad reached over the stall door and pulled a piece of straw from her hair. "I've spent a good two hours searching for you. I did not think you would seek asylum *here*."

Rynn shrugged slightly and exchanged looks with Falada. "We're…friends? I think?"

Falada twitched his muzzle but did not disagree.

"I will remember that for future reference." Conrad opened the stall door and motioned for Rynn to come out.

"Is something wrong?" Rynn asked. "Do you need me to speak against Lady Maela?"

"No," Conrad said. "It is merely that I believe I owe you an explanation." He offered his hand.

Rynn hesitantly placed her palm against his, fighting the desire to blush when he entwined his fingers with hers and tugged her over to a rectangular hay bale that was pushed to the side.

"You certainly don't owe me anything of the sort." Rynn sat down on the hay bale and was surprised when Conrad didn't release her hand. "I lied to you—and the royal family! I consider myself very blessed that everyone has been so understanding about the situation."

Conrad shrugged. "It wasn't your choice to get swept up into the situation. If Davina had applied herself at all, she could have spared you much suffering." He sounded slightly disgruntled as he glared at Rynn's feet.

"I see. What did you feel the need to explain?" Rynn asked.

"My actions—specifically why I posed as the goose boy," Conrad straightened up and gazed down the aisleway with a small frown. "By the banquet we had when you first arrived, I had worked out you were not, in fact, Davina—which was in no small part thanks to your subtle hints. I surmised you were not voluntarily acting as the stand in, and as I knew already that Lady Maela was foul, I thought you were perhaps her puppet. It took me another day to put together your strange reaction to the arrival and employment of the new goose girl before I decided to chase that lead."

"But you didn't want to be recognized, so you used your magic to appear younger?" Rynn asked.

Conrad nodded and finally met her gaze. "My goal was to wrestle information from Davina. I did not expect your visits—though they did help me cobble together a slight understanding of what had happened."

"I can't believe I didn't recognize you." Rynn scowled briefly. "Though in my defense, I did not think anyone in Farthendale was the recipient of a fairy gift."

"It's why I am the spymaster." Conrad sat down next to Rynn on the hay bale, which suddenly seemed quite small. "No one expects a man from Farthendale to be able to use magic."

"I see." Rynn would have knit her fingers together to give herself an excuse to avoid Conrad's gaze, but as he retained custody of her left hand, the most she could do was inspect the nails of her right hand. "I should have known something was up. You really were an awful goose boy."

"I assume you learned to care for geese as a child?" Conrad asked.

Rynn mutely nodded. *For all the good it did me. I just assumed the agriculture master was horrible at hiring new animal care-takers.*

Conrad was silent for several moments, then continued his story. "I had surmised that Lady Maela and Captain Hulderic would play their hand today and move against you—and Astoria. I wanted a clean explanation, which is why I spent the morning convincing Davina to come up to the palace to set the matter straight," Conrad continued.

"It took you the morning to bring her around?"

"No." Conrad's brow twitched in irritation. "She agreed to come almost immediately, but she insisted on washing, combing, and braiding her hair first."

Rynn covered her grinning lips with her free hand to keep from laughing and stirring up a wind. *She may be smarter than I gave her credit for, but she still is Davina after all...* Rynn cleared her throat. "I see. Thank you for the explanation. I am quite relieved to hear you mostly worked the mess out."

"We should have told you," Conrad said. "Uncle, Geraint, and I debated fiercely for days. They over-ruled me, of course."

Rynn blinked, surprised that it was Conrad who had voted to explain everything to her. *But their knowledge of the situation—or at least the knowledge that I was not the real Davina—explains some of their conduct. The royal family was always very kind, but after those first few days, they seemed to pull back from me and treat me more like a guest and less like a daughter-in-law.* Geraint in particular had pulled back —which was quite valiant of him, really, as it meant he was less familiar with her than even Conrad had been.

Conrad awkwardly cleared his throat in the silence, then continued. "They worried you wouldn't be able to properly act terrified if you knew we were aware of the situation and Hulderic tried to intimidate you. We needed Lady Maela to make active claims against the Astorian royal family, you see, before we could arrest her. Uncle worried you might accidentally tip off years of our clandestine work."

"They were right," she admitted. "I doubt I could have held my tongue and refrained from giving Lady Maela a verbal lashing if I knew what she was planning." Rynn smiled at the secretive spymaster.

Conrad was staring intently at her—or more specifically her lips. "Mmhmm," he said.

"I'm relieved it's all over," Rynn said.

"Right. Yes." Conrad slightly shook his head, as if clearing his thoughts. "On behalf of my Aunt and Uncle, I have been instructed to officially welcome you, Corynn, to Cadburey."

Ahh yes, they really are a kind family. Rynn smiled wistfully. "It's just Rynn."

"Did not Princess Davina refer to you as Corynn?"

"Davina has always called me by my full name, Corynn, but I do prefer Rynn."

"Very well, Rynn. Aunt Morgaine wishes for me to tell you that the rooms next to Davina's have been prepared for you."

Conrad—still holding Rynn's hand, which, frankly, was starting to grow hot—rested their joint hands on his thigh.

Rynn noticed when he stroked the top of her hand with his thumb, but she was still distracted by his words. "The quarters *next* to Davina? I'm sorry, but those must be too good for a mere lady's maid."

"You aren't a mere lady's maid. You are our guest," Conrad said.

"The original arrangement was that I am to serve as Davina's lady's maid until she is married and settled here, then I may return to Astoria," Rynn said.

The furrow was back in Conrad's brow. "You mean to leave?"

"Forgive me, but I did not plan to act as a lady's maid for the rest of my life—even if I did serve a princess," Rynn said, privately adding, *Indeed, I got this job knowing it was temporary. If I continued, I would probably suffocate Davina with a pillow within a year.*

"No one is expecting you to serve as a lady's maid," Conrad said. "Even Davina. She says you are her friend. Her only friend."

The words touched Rynn more than she cared to admit. As much as she complained about Davina and despaired over her impetuous actions, she *did* like the princess. When she wasn't dragging her into ridiculous messes, that was.

"*I* hoped you would stay in Farthendale," Conrad added.

"Why?" Rynn asked.

"Because I believe I am in love with you," Conrad said.

Rynn gaped at him. *Did he just...but I...what?* She mentally scrambled for a foothold, unused to being caught completely off guard.

Conrad used her stunned silence as a chance to stroke their clasped hands with his thumb. "I thought I was being imprudently obvious," he grunted. "Foolishly so. I would never hold hands with my cousin's intended, after all."

"I...I...I," she stammered, unable to come up with anything intelligent to say.

Conrad waited a few moments. "Do you find my confession distasteful?"

"Nooo!" Rynn said pulling back in horror. "Not at all! It's just...unexpected?"

Down the aisleway, Falada hung his head over his stall door and snorted. "In what way? You've had more romantic rendezvous than most engaged couples."

Rynn shot the fairy horse a glare. "Don't you have a mushroom to flirt with?"

Falada bared his teeth at her, and the horse and rider sneered at each other for several moments.

"You still have not given a reply," Conrad said.

He's not easily distracted, is he? Rynn primly cleared her throat. "Are you really sure about this?" she asked.

"Yes."

Rynn nodded slowly. "Right."

"Then will you stay?" Conrad asked. "For me?"

Rynn mutely nodded.

Conrad smiled—a true smile that made his eyes light up and softened his expression to make him handsome enough to rival his royal cousin. "Thank you."

He leaned in again, though this time he did not stop as he had before; instead, he pressed his lips to hers in a kiss.

Rynn was aware of his free hand cupping her cheek as he tugged her closer to him and deepened the kiss.

She wished the moment would last forever, but she broke off the kiss with a startled squeak when Falada kicked his stall door.

Conrad growled. "Yes?"

"I do not wish to see you noisy humans groping each other," Falada said. "Be gone."

Rynn grumbled under her breath and pushed her face into Conrad's shoulder.

The spymaster shrugged. "Fine."

Rynn blinked when he stood. "Fine? Fine wha—ahh!" She

broke off with a startled cry—which threw stall shavings into the air in little clouds when the wind reacted—as Conrad picked her up with ease. "What are you doing?"

"Taking you to the palace. I suppose I should officially introduce you to my parents with your real name," Conrad said.

"Um," Rynn intelligently replied.

Conrad briefly pressed his lips to her temple. "They'll love you," he said.

"That's reassuring," Rynn muttered as he carried her from the stable. She waved to Falada over his shoulder before they ducked out of the stable and into the crisp night air.

Rynn gazed up at the stars that studded the sky. *Is it just me, or are they brighter now?* She wrapped her arms around Conrad's neck. "You can put me down."

He nodded. "I could."

"...Allow me to rephrase that. You *should* put me down."

Conrad shrugged. "No."

"No?" Rynn repeated.

"Until today, I had to keep my distance—or at least I had to try to. It's no longer necessary, so, no."

Rynn snorted at his logic, but tightened her grip on his neck as she recalled the day's events and her near miss with Lady Maela.

Rynn had spent most of her life managing others—whether it was geese, her siblings, or Davina. She had always considered herself a workhorse who toiled for the sake of others. Hearing Conrad's story, *knowing* what he had done for her sake...

"Thank you, Conrad, for protecting me," she said suddenly.

"Of course. Whatever you desire." Conrad looked at her, his dark eyes glittering in the starlight. "I'll even be a goose boy if you wish."

"Please, *no*," Rynn said. "I like you much better as a man."

Conrad hesitated in the courtyard. "Maybe it *isn't* necessary to see my parents this evening," he said, his gaze heated as he again stared at Rynn's lips.

Rynn smacked him in the shoulder. "Conrad!"

"Is that a yes?"

"It's a *please put me down*."

"Request denied." Conrad again started for the palace.

Rynn leaned into his shoulder, her happiness building. *So, this is what I was missing after all.*

EPILOGUE

Rynn walked hand-in-hand with Conrad, grinning as she watched Falada snort and roll on the sweet grass of the goose meadow.

Conrad's horse—a mare as calm as Falada was temperamental —munched on grass nearby, occasionally raising her head to search for Conrad.

"I don't think I've ever seen Falada this happy before," Rynn said.

"I don't think anyone knew he was capable of *being* happy," Conrad said. "Which is why many questioned Davina's choice of gift."

After Conrad and Rynn had announced their relationship to Conrad's family, Davina had declared it was absolutely necessary to hold a double wedding—which would take place in one week—and gave Falada to Rynn as a gift. (Publicly, Queen Cassia was horrified Davina had given something so priceless to her one-time *lady's maid*, but privately everyone agreed it was a wise choice, particularly because Falada had broken down his stall door and started shouting for Rynn when a groom tried to saddle him for Davina to ride.)

"He didn't want to leave his home—back when the fairies first gave him to the Astorian royal family I mean," Rynn said. "I think he's been so callous because he had no control over his own life, even though he can talk and feel like you or I."

Conrad nodded and watched the fairy horse stand and toss his head. "It makes sense."

Rynn grinned as one of the braver geese waddled up to Falada and rubbed its head on his legs. Falada swatted the bird with his tail and walked away, the goose trailing in his wake.

Conrad kissed the top of Rynn's head and snaked an arm around her waist. "Was the letter you received from Eva this morning filled with good news?"

"Yes. She is finally happy—which she deserves after all she endured this past year. I thought I was in a poor situation, but at least I was not kidnapped." Rynn stooped over and picked up a dandelion that had already bloomed and was now a sphere of fluff and seeds. She blew, making the seeds scatter with her breath, then blinked when she realized the wind barely stirred.

"Is it...fading?" Rynn thought, afraid to hope. (Regulating her breathing had grown particularly difficult thanks to Conrad's habit of snatching random kisses from her.)

"Is what fading?" Conrad asked.

"My magic—controlling wind," Rynn stood and dusted her hands off before tucking her arm into Conrad's.

"Of course it's fading."

Rynn and Conrad whirled around to find Mortimer—his wings as small as ever and his clothes perhaps more rumpled than usual.

Mortimer raised an eyebrow and looked down his nose at Rynn. "I *said* it would only be temporary."

"Fairy Godfather Mortimer?" Conrad asked. (Rynn had, of course, told him the story of how she had received her unwanted powers.)

Mortimer squinted at Conrad. "You're not a prince." He

turned to Rynn. "He's not a prince. I thought all girls wanted to marry a prince."

"No," Rynn said firmly. "We don't."

"Picky, picky, picky. You don't want a prince; you don't want magic powers." Mortimer rolled his eyes and shook his head in disgust.

"So my powers really will fade?" Rynn asked, hardly able to contain her glee.

Mortimer scratched his ear. "Yeah. You've got about a week left with it."

"*Thank you.*" Rynn impulsively hugged the fairy godfather, making him squawk in disdain.

"*No* touching." Mortimer peeled her off and shivered in revulsion.

"I just didn't want it to be like..." Rynn trailed off, thinking of her siblings that had been granted magical gifts.

Mortimer dusted his robes off, his face still creased in disgust. "I might have learned my lesson. Until I haven't, anyway."

Rynn blinked. "What?"

"Nothing."

"Thank you for caring for my bride, sir," Conrad said, respectfully bowing. (Rynn had no idea how he did it without grimacing at the arrogant expression that settled on Mortimer's face. It was probably his training as a spy.)

"Of course. The oldest brat is my goddaughter...and all of that other disgusting sentimental garbage." Mortimer grunted, then shifted his gaze to Rynn. "You're fine now. Wish granted?"

Rynn reveled in the act of letting herself sigh and raising barely more than a whisper of a breeze. *Naturally he's most concerned with fulfilling wishes so he can get back to the research he's constantly yammering about.* "Yes, Mortimer. I'm very happy now. Thank you for your help," she said. Even though she wanted to shout and sic a goose on him, angering the fairy godfather wouldn't be a smart move.

Mortimer nodded once at Rynn and once at Conrad. "Good."

When the duo stared at him, he sneered. "Goodbye," then disappeared in his usual flash of light.

Rynn laughed when she was assured he was gone. "I'm going to be *free*! This is wonderful! I feel so happy I almost can't believe this all worked out. It's nearly too perfect!" She kissed Conrad on the cheek, laughing when he returned the favor by kissing her on the lips.

When they finally parted, Conrad studied her with a serious light in his eyes. "Are you satisfied living in Farthendale?" he asked.

She tilted her head. "What do you mean?"

Conrad furrowed his brow. "I know what your family means to you, and they *all* live in Astoria."

"Yes, well...the truth is I've fallen in love with Farthendale and its forests and mountains. Besides...you can leave Cadburey long enough that we could *visit* my family in Astoria, right?" Rynn propped her arms up on his shoulders, knitting her hands together behind the back of his neck.

"Of course," Conrad said. "If Geraint complains, we can always drag Lunette or Arthur with us and claim it is to further their education," he added, referring to his younger cousins.

Rynn grinned. "Excellent. I thought you would have a plan. So yes. I'm more than satisfied to live in Farthendale and to marry *you*."

"Good," Conrad nodded.

He kissed her again, this time releasing her only when Falada swore at a goose and galloped across the meadow to get away from it.

THE END

ENTWINED TALES

Everyone wishes they had a fairy godmother to make the world a little more magical...
They've never met Mortimer.

Every good deed merits a reward, at least according to the Fairy Council. But when a kind woodcutter's family is rewarded with a grumpy, sarcastic, irresponsible fairy godfather named Mortimer, their lives are changed forever... and not in a good way.

Follow the woodcutter's seven children as Corynn, Eva, Sophie, Elisette, Martin, Anneliese, and Penelope head out into the world to find adventure, new friends, and their very own happily-ever-afters. Their greatest challenge? Avoiding their fairy godfather's disastrous attempts to help.

Welcome to the Entwined Tales—six interconnected fairy tale retellings by authors KM Shea, Brittany Fichter, Shari L. Tapscott, Kenley Davidson, Aya Ling, and Melanie Cellier. Join the fun and enter the brand new world of the Entwined Tales for six enchanting stories filled with humor, magic, and romance.

Entwined Tales continues with Eva's Story:
An Unnatural Beanstalk:
A Retelling of Jack and the Beanstalk
by Brittany Fichter.

OTHER BOOKS BY K. M. SHEA

The Snow Queen:

Heart of Ice

Sacrifice

Snowflakes: A Snow Queen Short Story Collection

Timeless Fairy Tales:

Beauty and the Beast

The Wild Swans

Cinderella and the Colonel

Rumpelstiltskin

The Little Selkie

Puss in Boots

Swan Lake

Sleeping Beauty

Frog Prince

12 Dancing Princesses

Snow White

Three pack (Beauty and the Beast, The Wild Swans, Cinderella and the Colonel)

The Fairy Tale Enchantress:

Apprentice of Magic

Curse of Magic

The Elves of Lessa:

Red Rope of Fate

Royal Magic

King Arthur and Her Knights:

Enthroned

Enchanted

Embittered

Embark

Enlighten

Endeavor

Endings

Three pack 1 (Enthroned, Enchanted, Embittered)

Three pack 2 (Embark, Enlighten, Endeavor)

Robyn Hood:

A Girl's Tale

Fight for Freedom

The Magical Beings' Rehabilitation Center:

Vampires Drink Tomato Juice

Goblins Wear Suits

The Lost Files of the MBRC

Other Novels

Life Reader

Princess Ahira

A Goose Girl

Second Age of Retha: Written under pen name A. M. Sohma

The Luckless

The Desperate Quest

The Revived

ABOUT THE AUTHOR

K. M. Shea is a fantasy-romance author who never quite grew out of adventure books or fairy tales, and still searches closets in hopes of stumbling into Narnia. She is addicted to sweet romances, witty characters, and happy endings. She also writes LitRPG and GameLit under the pen name, A. M. Sohma.

Printed in Great Britain
by Amazon

42583188R00069